NOW THAT YOU'RE BACK

A.L.Kennedy was born in Dundee in 1965. Her first collection of stories, *Night Geometry and the Garscadden Trains*, won the Saltire Award for Best First Book, a Scottish Arts Council Book Award, and the *Mail On Sunday*/John Llewellyn Rhys Prize. She has also published a novel, *Looking for the Possible Dance*, which won a Somerset Maugham Award, and a second collection of short stories, *Now That You're Back*. In 1993 she was chosen as one of the twenty Best of Young British Novelists. She lives and works in Glasgow. Her new novel, *So I Am Glad*, is published by Jonathan Cape.

BY A.L. KENNEDY

Night Geometry And The Garscadden Trains
Looking For The Possible Dance
Now That You're Back
So I Am Glad

A.L. Kennedy

NOW THAT YOU'RE BACK

V

VINTAGE

Published by Vintage 1995

2 4 6 8 10 9 7 5 3 1

These stories previously appeared in the following publications:
'A Perfect Possession' in *Chapman Magazine*;
'Warming My Hands and Telling Lies' and
'On Having More Sense' in *NWS* 9 & 10;
'Failing to Fall' in *Granta* 43; and 'Friday Payday' in
Original Prints 4.

First published in Great Britain by
Jonathan Cape Ltd, 1994

Vintage
Random House, 20 Vauxhall Bridge Road, London SW1V 2SA

Random House Australia (Pty) Limited
20 Alfred Street, Milsons Point, Sydney
New South Wales 2061, Australia

Random House New Zealand Limited
18 Poland Road, Glenfield,
Auckland 10, New Zealand

Random House South Africa (Pty) Limited
PO Box 337, Bergvlei, South Africa

Random House UK Limited Reg. No. 954009

A CIP catalogue record for this book
is available from the British Library

ISBN 0 09 945711 3

Papers used by Random House UK Ltd are natural,
recyclable products made from wood grown in sustain-
able forests. The manufacturing processes conform to
the environmental regulations of the country of origin

Printed and bound in Great Britain by
Cox & Wyman, Reading, Berkshire

For E. M. Kennedy, M. Price, J. H. Price,
my family and friends who rarely fail,
with thanks to Bob Kingdom.

CONTENTS

A Perfect Possession

IT HURTS WHEN we love somebody, because loving is a painful thing, that is its nature. Today, even though we are not sure that the pain will pass, it has to be said that our loving is hurting us.

He is spending this evening in his room where we don't see him. It is raining outside and he always likes to smell the rain. Often, we have listened while he opens his window and lets in the damp and the insects and the draught. Downstairs, we can hear the rasp of wood when he tugs at the frame. He can be strong sometimes, even though he is small, and the window is loose fitting and old, he can push it up quite easily. So he empties out the heat we pay for and he really doesn't think. We don't know where he gets that from, his terrible lack of thought, he simply isn't one bit like us.

Of course, no little boy likes to think and we expect to do that for him until he is grown and responsible. This is a burden to us, but a light and pleasant one. Loving someone means that you will do things for them, almost without consideration. We would catch him if he ran and fell, we would bandage him if he were bleeding and now we can measure his actions and think ahead on his behalf. On many occasions, we can stop him being hurt.

We don't think of these attentions as any kind of chore, after all, when he was so noisy and smelly and dirty, so very difficult to hold, we didn't abandon him. We knew he was a baby, not just some troublesome pet, and we kept him with us. For months, he made our lives extremely different, in fact he was quite a tyrant, but we didn't mind. We taught him to do better. Now we can really believe that he is quiet and clean as a matter of course. He sometimes makes mistakes, but then, mistakes are how we teach him. We learned by being corrected and that is the best way.

The worry of keeping him safe is another matter, that can be draining now and then. For example, we didn't know what to do about his window. He might have opened it up and then dropped out, so we had the bars put on, but still we had to fret because a fire could easily trap him in his room, what with his door being locked the way it must. Then there was the problem of his still opening the window inside the bars and doing whatever odd little boy things he feels himself moved to do. His carelessness could have left us with rot in the window frame and perhaps he would catch cold. It was much better to screw down the window and put our minds at rest, because he will give us promises and then break them, which hurts us all in the end. Better to use the woodscrews than tempt him to lie at us.

4

He wasn't grateful for what we did, but that is very normal in boys; we understand. His spite didn't stop us saying that if he ever were in difficulties, or a fire did occur, he could bang on his door the way he does now and we would certainly let him out.

We are puzzled he still prefers not to be granted full run of the house. We don't know how many times we've asked him if he would like to be trusted not to break anything else, or to disturb us. Always he refuses the privilege, which we suppose shows that he knows his limitations: he is still dreadfully clumsy for his age. We make a point of sharing meals with him and having him sit at our table — it is so important he should have good eating manners when he goes to school. We suffer for the decision, but we persevere. It doesn't matter how many glasses he drops and the stains he makes in the tablecloth don't deter us; we will stop the silly shaking in his hands and eventually see him performing respectably.

If we let the child know our rules and what happens when he breaks them, it's only a matter of time until everything falls into place. More people should understand that and keep the incoming flood of modern and imported attitudes out of their homes. Today we all suffer at the hands of criminals created by sloppy care. A good child will be a good citizen and a bad child will not, as anyone can appreciate. Upbringing has to be just that — bringing up from the animal level to something higher, better, closer to God. Obviously, some races will always be nearer the animal than others, we must accept this as God's will, but if everyone would simply do their best then how much more pleasant the world would soon become. As it is, we are almost afraid to go out.

He never goes out without us, of course, we can't trust him to strangers. This means we must be with him always which takes time and effort, but we would rather do a good job now than reap the sour rewards for idleness and slacking later. We tell him this and expect him to feel the same. Equally, we wouldn't leave him to the tender mercies of the television. If we sat him in front of an endless stream of filthy music and filthy talk, filthy actions, what would we get? We would get a filthy boy. He may listen to some radio, look at his picture book or amuse himself in any way he likes and enjoy the haven we have made for him. Our home is a clean home, free from tabloid sewage and the cheap and foreign pollution most people seem content to have wash around them all the day. We are not like that, we even sing him hymns to keep the air sweet in our rooms. It's such a pity we can't take him out to church.

We have the cares and troubles that come with the gift of a child. It would be very easy to give him material things and think that making him happy would make him good. There was even a time when we did offer him presents, wholesome gifts for a boy, and we were surprised when he broke them, or dirtied them, or pushed

6

them aside. He could quickly forget we had given him anything.

This ingratitude and forgetfulness was hurtful, but because we love him, it hurt us even more to take the things away. Still, we have the bitter satisfaction of finding our judgements proved right. His will is undeveloped and can be swiftly poisoned by exposure to the material side of this world. A time came when he wanted something he could hug on to in the night and we knew what that meant. That was a warning. We had to take his pillow away because he would sleep alongside of it, in spite of what we told him, and that was dirty, that was more of the filth we constantly fight to save him from. It grieved us when he cried about it, cried in the night, and didn't understand the procedures to which he would have to conform. In the end he was persuaded to pray with us and became peaceful which was a little victory for us all.

Other victories will come. We would love him to have birthdays and presents like other children. That would be such fun, but the way he is now, it would be quite impossible. We hope that he will change in time and become more upright and mannerly, a suitable example to others, and we are overjoyed to see that he is already much quieter than he ever has been. Sometimes we only know he's there, because of a certain feeling in the house and the ties that loving binds.

His extreme delicacy frightens us, naturally. Some mornings when we look at him, he seems so pale and thin, perhaps as an angel might be. His whole body is almost white which is clean, but not natural. No matter what we do, what methods we apply, he turns back to white again within days or hours, even minutes. He could have gone to school this term, had he been well, but we will have to wait until he's stronger and perhaps reconcile ourselves to the likelihood that he may never go to a normal school. That would be a disappointment. That would make us sad.

Sometimes we have to ask ourselves if he is a judgement on us for our part in his conception. Children come from sin, they are the immediate flower of sin and there is sin in him. It would be idle to consider why this should be so and we believe only that, through him, we may find an opportunity to conquer sin again and again. This is more a privilege than a punishment and we treasure it. Many times in the night, we examine him for signs of filthiness, wetness of every kind, and often we are given cause for concern, or rather, we are challenged by sin. He has bad seed in him and it comes out. Evil cannot help but flaunt itself and in the darkness it is most free to be manifest. How weary he makes us, forcing us to search and watch and search: a rubber sheet is not enough, an alarm is not enough, all our vigilance is not enough. Nobody knows what pains we have to take with the boy, purely to keep him up and away from his animal self.

And the animal brings on the animal, the beast. We find him tempting us as the devil tried to tempt Our Lord and we are uncovered as wanting. He offers us what he has and should not have and takes advantage of our tiredness, our weakness and our humanity.

We have to be strong for his sake, we have to pray and take action fearlessly for the sake of all our souls because we want him to grow up into a man we will be proud of. He will not be a fear and a stranger in our house because our strength and fortitude will not allow it.

Even tonight, when we think of our love for him and feel tender, we are undefeated because we know that tenderness is not enough. We must call upon our action and our faith and, with God's guidance, proceed.

Our child has sinned today. He has summoned an evil under our roof. What sin, what evil, need not be mentioned, we will not dignify it with a name. We need only say that he is ugly with sin and now we must call upon our God-given love to claim him for beauty so that good may triumph in all our hearts. We will release him from himself and hear him thank us for it. We must.

Time after time and time out of time, we will purify him for the coming world and watch him cultivate his gratitude, piece by piece. When we are finished, he will be a good boy entirely.

CHRISTINE

I CAN HARDLY describe the way she was at school. That's where I first knew her – at school. She was in the year above me, but there was something that looked much younger inside her eyes which would make you feel either protective or embarrassed depending on where you met her and what she did.

What she did best was falling over. If I try to picture her then, all I can see are badly adjusted ankles and lean, tapering feet, knees and elbows all slightly out of control. A few of us, because we were boys and therefore nasty, placed bets through the whole of one week against Christine once being able to walk clear across the playground without at least tripping up. Large spaces with no apparent obstacles seemed to confuse her. She would stand by the railings every morning like a freshly liberated convict and then painstake her way up the tarmac, redefining clumsy as she went.

I bet on her for eight minor stumbles and one wholesale collapse. She didn't let me down, but the money I won made me blush whenever I saw her. She tended to make me feel guilty. In fact, it seems now that knowing

Christine has gradually introduced me to every kind of guilt. I can't dislike her for it. She was just there while I did what I wanted, gently overlooking all the ungentle things I thought were safely hidden in my head.

Whether she was attractive then would be difficult to say; she always appeared in a flurry of doomed objects and bleeding which made her very difficult to see. And she could also be emotionally distracting. This was a time when anyone could bleed in public without becoming a source of general alarm, but Christine was still unnerving. She would manifest herself in classrooms like a schoolgirl saint, coyly displaying her latest gashes with a quietly knowing smile. She had an air of gory intimacy that I've only ever met again in some religious paintings – those chummy anatomical snapshots certain artists are moved to conjure up from martyrdoms. I've often considered that martyrdom could become almost bearable if it wasn't so terribly over-exposed – God makes a dreadful agent, all publicity and never mind the pain. But I have to admit, the images are striking in just the way that Christine was, she shared the same kind of culinary fascination.

All of which made her exciting in a way that schools do not encourage. She seemed so greedy for disaster that there could be nothing left for us. As children went, we were all miraculously fortunate and dexterous. From around a corner or behind a door we would hear a light kind of whoop and perhaps an impact and that would be Christine, collecting another proof of physical disinterest.

She saved us the trouble; any trouble. And any guilt on our part was largely dispersed by the knowledge that she was never punished for the so obviously innocent chaos she kept in tow. Still, it never seemed wise to cultivate her company – no one hugs a lightning conductor, you just leave it outside to do its job. In other words, she was hard not to notice, but never a friend and in no way a person I made the slightest effort to remember. When I left school, I had no intention of seeing, or thinking about her again. One way and another, I'm not much of a one for keeping in touch.

I went to a university in England and came back home as little as possible, because I could no longer be at home there. Scots down south either turn into Rob Roy McStrathspeyandreel or simply become Glaswegian – no one will understand you, if you don't. Rather than smile through a lifetime of simpleton assumptions and kind enquiries after Sauchiehall Street in the frail hope of one day explaining my existence, I chose to be English and to disappear.

Like many of us, I already had a variety of accents for private and social use. I found it remarkably easy to sound like almost anyone I met. In fact ease had very little to do with it – I would echo whoever I spoke to quite automatically, moving from neutral to bland imitation and back again. Today this makes all situations alike to me – I am consistently slightly out of place, but never uncomfortably so. And if we are ever stuck for conversation people can always ask me where I come from and I can always fail to answer them.

I already had my first job, doing it doesn't matter what, when Christine reappeared. At that time I had found myself sucked into a knot of more or less convincing Scots abroad and she was brought to me by another depressing feature of expatriate life – the fraternal gathering. Visiting them en masse was precisely like returning to almost any small home town. After a space of no matter how many years, you will meet at least one person you went to school with, one person on intimate terms with a distant and notorious relative and one person whom you never wished to see or think about again. For a variety of reasons Christine qualified on all counts and one particular night she was inevitably there.

We were both at a party where the proportions of food and drink most likely to produce a pleasant evening had been exactly reversed and I knew it was her, but then I didn't.

She was older, obviously, but still very much as I suddenly found I could remember, only she wasn't Christine. There was something wrong. Slim, long boned with a satisfactory skin and fine hair: all was as it should have been, until I noticed her eyes. I could see into her eyes. Christine was looking directly at me, her head and body were still and she was at rest. I was seeing her for the first time fully in focus and a woman and finding that was quite a combination. She smiled, perhaps because I may have been smiling too, then turned back to the man beside her and whatever space we had occupied together ceased to exist. I felt a touch insulted which surprised me.

Perhaps an hour or two later Christine came out of the sun to speak to me. I mean by this that she appeared from a kind of blind spot in the manner of enemy aircraft, or possibly angels descending – I simply didn't see her until she was already there beside me. It suddenly seemed that we must have been right in the middle of talking and something had interrupted us, possibly decades ago, but now it didn't matter because we were back together and things were fine again. I'm mentioning this because although I knew that hadn't happened, her manner convinced me it was true.

'You shouldn't be upset. He's a friend of my mother's and a very nice man.'

'I wasn't upset.'

Well there wouldn't have been any point to pretending I didn't know what she meant. There was also no point in lying, but I did it anyway.

'No, I wasn't upset at all.'

'I'm sorry, I thought you were. I must have been mistaken. How have you been?'

'Oh, fine.'

And it made sense to say that, as if the years we hadn't seen each other had made us better acquainted.

'We have a progressive friendship, then.'

'I'm sorry, I don't know what you mean, Christine. I even . . . you are Christine?'

'Yes, I'm always Christine. I meant we have a friendship of the kind that progresses without us. We hardly spoke when I knew you at school and now we seem almost conversational. I find that happens a lot; the less you see each other, the more you get. The best kind of marriages might be like that, what do you think?'

'I think they might very well be like that. But you're not married? Divorced?'

'No, I'm not. Not either. I like your voice the way you have it now. It's only a little bit odd. Do you speak to yourself that way?'

'If I speak to myself in the first place. I don't think I'd admit to that.'

'Inside your head, that's where people talk to themselves. What's your car like?'

'Red. Undisturbed, I hope. It's outside my flat. I walked here.'

'Mm.'

And I wanted to walk with her then. I thought the most pleasant thing at that moment in the world would be the exercise of strolling through orange-grey drizzle and looking in at windows with Christine close enough for the unaccidental brush of shoulder and hip. The idea of it all was so strong that for a little while I had to close my eyes. When I glanced at her again she was smiling and waving to someone behind me. I looked at the blue of the veins in her wrist, the rose-coloured ends of her fingers. She looked at me.

'I'm staying with Shona, you don't know her.'

'Shona.'

'You don't know her, but I'm staying at her house and I said I would be back early. I'm walking there now. You can keep me company.'

I'm not an especially sheltered person, I don't lead an impoverished life of solitary card games and lonely trips to cinema matinées. I am not in the habit of recalling in palpable detail, every moment of every uneventful walk along ragged pavements under autumn rain that I have made with man, woman, child or domestic pet. But walking with Christine was special even before it happened. Everything was heightened. I was heightened. The feel of the air when I inhaled was heightened, was almost overwhelming, in fact. I wasn't sure if I could bear to move. It was all very singular.

There is, I know, nothing more tedious than second-hand enthusiasm. I won't describe every garden gate and every shadow as we passed them, the wonderful effect of the fish and chicken bar's illuminated sign as it fell and rolled on the slick of the paving. Instead, I will bring us all to the end of the journey and the brick terraced house where Shona lived. You will take it for granted that the bricks and the terrace and the house were all imbued with an indescribable quality the like of which I had never before encountered.

I am standing, as I stand sometimes now in daydreams, with my back to the street and my front to Christine who is gently insinuating the spare key that Shona gave her into the front door lock. This is a very Freudian moment. I have temporarily forgotten how to inhale, but this does not disturb me as inhaling is no longer necessary.

Christine opens the door with a dull exhalation of hallway and we both see a dim smirr of light from the top of the stair and the loom of various furnishings. I notice that I am steadying myself by bracing one hand up against the door frame.

Christine inclines her head to me, smiles and with a gesture I find quite confusing at first, presses her thumb lightly across my lips from top to bottom, making a little seal just below my nose. I want to sob, or something very like that, but listen to her voice instead.

'Good night, then. I hope you have a safe journey home. It isn't far if you take that other road there to the left. And – '

She slides the palm of her other hand along my arm from the shoulder to the elbow, where it rests.

'Just to let you know, you are thinking "That feels nice. I don't know what this is could I come in Durex Elite – where were they – blue packet a picture of her standing and wearing a cream silk petticoat and nothing else God nothing else the light in another woman's face – what

was her name – this wouldn't be like that there is something very odd about this house – what would she feel
like to be inside of – where else will she look – not in
there you mustn't think it no not that but imagine snug
very snug I can imagine her tits they would be marvellous edible shut up impossible dream joke wicked all this
stuff reeling out like a prick like a rope not like a prick
I don't have a prick like a rope God the white light of
hitting something. What is this?" Sorry. I don't mean
to pry.'

I had to grip her arm to keep myself from stumbling.
I had never heard anyone say my thoughts out, word for
word, including the punctuation. That hadn't happened
before. I believe that things like it do not often occur. It
was a shock. It was an invasion. I have never liked people
telling me the way they guess I'm thinking – that feels
oppressive and sly and is tediously inaccurate. Someone
telling me precisely what I am thinking, beat by beat –
that seems to affect my soul.

'But I can't see your soul, only how you picture it. I'm
sorry if I frightened you. You seemed so lonely, I only
wanted to say hi.'

'There are places where I like to be alone.'

'Partly it was selfish, too. I needed someone to know
why I had to be the way you remember when I was
young. And you remember so clearly, I wanted you to
know what made me fall so often, have so many accidents.

You see it's very distracting, hearing what everyone thinks all the time. It took me years to get used to it.'

'You can do this to everyone.'

'Of course, I can't help it.'

She gave a slight frown and squeezed my hand.

'I can't answer any of your other questions. You know my secret and I know all of yours, but we can keep secrets. I know we're both very good at that. You'll have to go now, but don't worry about getting home, you'll manage far better than you imagine. I'm sure we will meet again, but I don't suppose it will be soon. I am going away from here tomorrow. Do take care. I have your number now – yes, I do – so I may call you. God bless.'

Do you know what that made me do, most of all? Nothing histrionic – no screaming or obsession, paranoia – no, I simply found myself wondering how clean I really was. If someone chose to walk around inside me, how much of it would I be happy for them to see?

I did get home, but I wasn't alright. I was full of untidy corners and pieces of dark.

I have never been one for confessions, for cleaning house, as our American friends would say, so for a number of months I felt decidedly uncomfortable. This did, however, eventually fade. I have found in my life that many uncomfortable things do just slip away, although I might never imagine that they could. It is almost better that I should have more and more unpleasant experiences so they can wear me into a deeper and deeper ease. This goes against popular logic, but has for many years had a practical value I find it difficult to overestimate.

I wouldn't mention anything too unpalatable from my past, because it would serve no particular purpose, other than to cause disturbance. Still, there was one incident I would like to mention, because it concerns Christine.

That day had not been lucky. A great deal had gone wrong and I was worried about a colleague of mine. I don't normally work with others very closely – I don't have that kind of job, or that kind of nature – but sometimes there will be a person who acts with me as what I might call a colleague. That day had ended with my colleague in serious trouble and I was feeling tired and irresponsible and guilty. I was at home, lying across an armchair and discovering I could not relax. Having started tight, I was simply drinking myself tighter, if that makes any sense.

When my telephone rang I answered it, expecting to be threatened, or fired, or cursed in some appropriate way.

'Hello, this is Christine. I can't talk for long.'

'What?'

'It's very difficult to hear what you're thinking when you're drunk. I would have waited until the morning, but I began to be confused about what you might do.'

'Christine? You can't – it's been years. Over this distance?'

'Of course over this distance, if I want to. I would

recognise you anywhere. And, to be honest we seem to be sympathetic. You've been shouting at me all week.'

'Where have you been?'

'That doesn't matter, somewhere away, somewhere I can reach out from if I want to hear, but otherwise not. You're the only thing that's disturbed me in a long while. Do go to sleep. You would sleep if you tried to.'

'But you don't know – '

'Don't be silly. I know, I know about the week in September, I know about Belgian fast food. I know.'

'Alright. Keep it safe.'

'Everything is safe. Everything is alright. Have a bath and go to bed and think about leaving.'

'What?'

'You heard. No more work – do something good for yourself. Stop hurting. It is possible. Go to bed. I'll be thinking of you.'

Naturally, I didn't go to bed. Christine had been right, though, I did sleep very soon after her call and stayed well under for twenty hours, or so.

When I finally came to, the armchair had wrecked my back, but my head was relatively stable. I could remember very little of what Christine had said – only the feeling her voice had given me was clear. That morning I found it impossible to feel as unaccompanied as usual and there was a pleasant sensitivity in my chest, a sort of warmth, that lasted almost until lunch time. I think that was to do with her.

What came next didn't make any sense until I saw Christine again, I believe for the very last time. I would take any amount of steps to prove myself wrong, to speak to her and watch her eyes, reading off the inside of my skull, but I know it won't happen. My efforts would be wasted and, more importantly, would disturb her so I don't make them.

I was in London and it was last year at the start of autumn. There was a dull mist crawling hand in glove over the car roofs and making my mouth taste of lead. I exhaled as I walked, adding a little more to the general cloud.

This all seemed entirely appropriate. I was cleaning up the details to close my final piece of work and when it was over, both I and the mist could be gone. For now, no one could really see me. I and the other pedestrians all muffled along between polished housefronts – carrot cake brick and bicycles and Banham burglar alarms. It is difficult in this district to tell agencies from embassies from residences from hotels and I have always liked it because no one can really belong here – we all of us just come and go.

Behind a little corner church there was a yard or two of garden, safely fenced and locked away from passing strangers and equipped with a range of printed regulations governing its legal use. Of course, when I glanced towards a flicker of light through the chainlink, Christine was there. She was dressed as a nun.

'I *am* a nun.'

'Christine. How are you, how are you here?'

'I'm very well. I have been given a way of living peacefully now. No, it's not at all like prison, I have a pattern to be free inside of and calm. Having a gift – like my gift – it isn't just a matter of receiving, you need help to find out just what you should do with it. It's nice to see you. I wasn't sure if you would pass here, but I hoped you might.'

'Shouldn't you be . . .'

'Somewhere else? No, my order sent me here, or very near here and sometimes I take advantage of this garden. I'm not a resident and I shouldn't have a key, but nobody minds me – nobody minds a little nun.'

'I'll take your word for it.'

'You can. Have you finished your business?'

'Yes, I have.'

'That's good. Then you can be free, too. Don't worry.'

'But a nun, that's so extreme.'

'No, it doesn't have to be. I'm not a very extreme nun. Are you sleeping better?'

'I sleep very well, never better.'

'That's nice. I do think about you, you know. You lead such a very uncomfortable life and I think about that. You could be as comfortable as me.'

'Marry and settle down, you mean?'

'How could you do that when the only woman who ever knew you is a nun?'

'The only woman who ever knew how to make me blush.'

'I'm sorry, I didn't intend to.'

I can't be absolutely sure of how long we talked, or of everything we said. The mist had seeped through my coat by the time Christine said she should go. She smiled and held my hand between hers. Her fingers made a fit no one else had managed.

'You have clean hands, a gentleman's hands.'

'But I'm not a gentleman.'

'Oh, you are in your heart, though. Take good care of yourself and remember you aren't alone. Really, you aren't.'

'You'll be praying for me, eh?'

'Of course, I always pray for cynics because they won't like it. It serves them right. But tell me what you see when you fall asleep.'

'My dreams, you mean?'

'No. Think of what you see just before you slip under. Yes, there you are.'

I found myself closing my eyes and watching a large, orange red flower, slowly uncurling a fist of petals under dew, round and round and in and in towards its heart. I knew what the heart would look like. I had seen it before.

'I send you that, didn't you know? Because you need

your sleep. I do have to go away now and we won't have each other's company again, but that's what you'll see every night. This way you'll know that I'm well and still thinking of you. You'll know you're not alone, which I think you need. Most people do. I will miss talking to you — it's always such a relief to not have to pretend.'

She left me with a misty kiss on my forehead and a chance to find out that her skin still smelt the same.

And now I am a dream man, you could say. Wherever I happen to be, I wait for my nights and that particular rest they bring me beyond what my body needs. Recently I have begun to worry that she may leave me. Perhaps there will be an accident or an illness I know nothing of until I look into an empty night and know she has gone.

I have a feeling this is something that Christine intended. Certainly, she will know I have started praying — only God would know to what. I pray that she will outlive me, that she doesn't forget me and that she will always be well. And sometimes I ask if the flower could be mine, really mine, to stay here just because of me. I wonder if that offends her, I don't mean it to.

On Having More Sense

AND LO, THE Wise Old Man spake forth unto the other, more lowly persons gathered symmetrically about him.

'Persons,' he said, 'Be it known that certain deep and significant Boons shall be granted upon you this day and at my hand. And some of these I shall enumerate to you now, lest they go forth unnoticed and generally unappreciated in the greater world beyond.

'Listen and wonder. You shall be granted the Power to cause previously stolid baked goods to rise upon every possible occasion.

'Also the Power of swimming in water.

'Also the Boon of being henceforth forever free from ill-defined but nonetheless annoying sore throats in combination with slight catarrh.'

And a lesser person did interrupt the sage discourse at this point and enquire with a discernibly cynical tone, 'And what is the difference between a Boon and a Power, Wise Old Man?'

And the Wise Old Man replied thusly. 'If thou knewest the difference between a Boon and a Power, thou wouldst not ask it. Thou mightst also know that it's rude to butt in.'

The Wise Old Man did then carefully wink his left eye in a rather jovial manner and continue.

'Know also that thou hast, even now, the inexpressible Boon of inhaling and exhaling most proficiently and without further instruction until the very moment of thy passing from this life into something different but equally interesting.'

And seating himself comfortably among the roots of his most particularly favourite tree the Wise Old Man did then look around him slowly, measuring the qualities of each face he saw while his companions did endeavour quite unsuccessfully to lower themselves into positions in which they could not be in any way more elevated than their chosen Sage. When they had all lain themselves upon the leaves and earth and irritating little sticks the Wise Old Man motioned them to sit up and behave sensibly like men and women rather than door stops.

'For now I must tell you the very heart and kernel of my life's philosophy after which I shall retire to my cave in the mountains and be seen no more. Yes, my little brothers and my little sisters this very day I will give you the key to my unassailable happiness. Use it well and don't forget a word, because it shall only pass into written form many years after our deaths and will, by then, be prey to all kinds of editorial intrusion.

'So hear now all those who look upon the world for

wonders, all those who would touch miracles and light, lower your eyes and close them and see what I say. The earthly paradise you seek is closer by far than you could know and guarded by a host of noble birds. Set your gaze upon those birds, oh my little sisters and my little brothers, let your minds and hearts be filled with the image and illumination, with the whirling, alchemical spirit of the penguin.

'No, you are not mistaken, behold the penguin. Admit neither a flinch, nor a flicker, hold fast to that reliably waddling figure and all will be well. Trust in me as you would trust a penguin, for which of you in the privacy of your soul may ever say you were betrayed by any penguin? Well then, slip your hands into the steady flippers of this paragon of birds and make ready to learn the superlative joys of its path.

'At this juncture it may be a man will cry out, "But, Wise Old Man, what am I to a penguin and what is a penguin to me? Penguins can't even whistle – which is odd in a bird – and they are, besides, foolishly short and very far from being an every day part of my life. I am not, after all, a zoo keeper."

'My answer is as clear as sunrise, but conveniently smaller. Perhaps you may feel you are distant from the penguin, does this mean you can take no delight in it? When your love is separated from you and in another place, will you cease to love? When you know the stars are untold miles away and not painted on a close roof of a sky, will they no longer glimmer and give joy? As you say, you are not the penguin's keeper – no man can truly be a penguin's keeper – but still you may appreciate the closeness of your heart and that of your avian exemplar. Hear the voice of the penguin in your mind and discover that there is no separateness in the world. You are part of the prisoner in his chains, part of the platypus, part of the statesman, the murderer and the tree. See yourself in all things which have the quality of being and show a little respect for the miracle this is.

'Little brothers and little sisters, think of the other distances in your lives. Think of the fears you have made into countries and think of the penguin, diving and mingling in ferocious oceans without a boundary or a care. You too may be bold and recognise a place for yourselves anywhere and everywhere in the great sea of humanity. You need never lose yourself and you will always be at home if you will simply emulate the penguin who combines the courtesy of the stranger with the ease of the friend no matter where it finds itself. It is not a matter of chance that no city has ever been besieged by penguins, that no international incident has ever been ignited by penguins, that no glistering genocidal design has ever been pursued by penguins. Remember this maxim on all occasions – Penguins Have More Sense.

'Here, I may point out that even the most sceptical persons may find something beneficial to learn from the penguin's example. One may discover, for instance, that good things may be sought out and found most easily with the generous assistance of reflection. If a man seeks to be near a penguin, he may transport himself across the globe to sit with one on the great ice. Or he may go to the zoo and find one there. He may judge for himself which is the more simple task.

'Now perhaps a woman may ask, "How can there truly be untold wonders concealed in such an unappetising, fishy creature – incapable of even peeling an apple for itself?"

'My answer is short as the penguin itself. Wonders there are. For is not the penguin a bird and yet does it not fly in water and not in air, teaching us that all is possible? You may see how will and water have smoothed and narrowed the natural feathers of any common bird into the almostfur of a penguin, clothing it perfectly against the snow and tempests of its chosen home. The feet of the penguin, though forever naked against such terrible things as icebergs and the bitterness of cold, salt sea, never trouble it for a moment, so fitted are they for their purpose. How equally fit are its wings for swimming, its beak for beaking, its bright eyes for discerning white across white. Thus the penguin teaches us of the full rightness and kindness of our world. Deny your relatives and friends, your teachers, the queer twist in your stomach when you wake with the dawn, inexcusably alive again – even to you, the world may be kind.

'The penguin will also show us that to stray without

forethought into unknown places may bring us griefs we never dreamed of. Imagine the penguin's torment if it was, all at once, arboreally inclined; its pitiful scrambles at mighty trunks, its patterings off leafy branches, its feeble beakings at slippery fruit. What would become of the penguin lost in forests, or indeed, in the rasp and wither of Ghobi sands? Before we begin our own momentous movements and translations we must be sure to equip ourselves for that which may reasonably befall. Preparedness is all and we may draw huge comfort from the fact that a penguin with a rope and crampons may indeed climb a tree, if not a mountain.

'An ignorant person may call to mind that the penguin has no money, neither clothing, nor true shelter and yet it lives a full and marvellous life, exactly suited to its nature. This is all very well for the penguin, but as men and women, we must always be aware that we, though bound in our souls with a sympathy for the penguin, are not ourselves in any way penguins. For the sake of your own existence, whenever and wherever it is in your power, let no human be placed in the position of a penguin. Above all let none of your kind be driven to lose those sustaining elements of character from which the penguin draws its strength — namely dignity, time, space and purpose.

'Little brothers and little sisters, allow yourselves to aspire to the penguin's joy. Have we not seen it slip with its fellows down its icy slides to bob in the sea, then gaily scramble up to slip again? It will clatter beaks and run in the wind with a light heart. A penguin finds no difficulty in being a penguin, it simply is. This also is possible for you.

'We may also take comfort in the fact that the penguin is not perfect, it merely does its best. Having chosen, perhaps less than wisely, to live somewhere at once movingly picturesque and tragically rich in rheumatic and sinus complaints, offering a diet composed almost exclusively of fish, many penguins have taken note of their mistake and acted upon it. Despite the lightness and satisfaction of its wintery life and plain fair at home, the penguin may be seen across the globe from Spain to California in zoological gardens where it may lounge in the sun, hail observing humanity and perhaps enjoy the luxury of peeled prawns, cabbage or drinking chocolate.

'You who are accustomed to the delights of all the above may learn humility when you examine your diet more closely. Even the littlest child cannot be unmoved when it taps the simplest egg at breakfast and then considers that this very egg might have brought forth a whole, new penguin; bold and free. Perhaps the egg had, in reality, only hidden the start of a chicken or a duck — even so, you may well be grateful that you were not born a chicken or a duck, nor yet boiled to make a breakfast. It is a sad and shameful fact that men have fed upon penguins in dark hours. You cannot help but be grateful that penguins have never been moved to feed upon men.

Humbled by your former wickedness you can be determined to bar the advent of any like abomination. If ever the difficulties of your life seem overwhelming, consider the prospect of being eaten alive by savage penguins and rejoice that such horrors are unknown to you.

'Now gaze for an instant upon the land of the penguin; the white, flat white of the penguin's home; and now let your eye fall upon the plumage of the penguin. "How can it be that the penguin is both white and black?" a keen mind may inwardly ask. "What may this signify?" One might suppose that, like the polar bear, like igloos, like milk, the penguin should be wholly white that it might be rendered safely invisible in its cold surrounds. But no, things are quite otherwise and they are so with a purpose.

'Notice that if the penguin should lie upon its face, turning its back upon the whole arc of the world, only the blackness of its feathers may be seen, marking out the glorious bird and exposing it entirely to foes of every kind. And yet, should the penguin lie upon its back, bearing its vital organs and the red tenderness of its heart to all that come, then is the whiteness of its belly feathers lost in the whiteness of the snow. Thus does the penguin, in embracing Nature, find itself protected by that very Nature and gentle Power which surrounds it. Embrace life freely, then, and see how freely it returns your favour, being ever mindful that a penguin does not often lie down, in either direction.

'Oh, think of the bitter winds in the penguin's feathers:

that sound you may never hear, but may imagine. Know that there is nothing you may not learn, in putting yourselves within the triangular webprints of the noble and courageous penguin. What goodness and example may you not find there? Name me the penguin which has ever burned down a listed building by carelessly smoking in bed? Point me out the mocker of elderly ladies, the jumper of queues, the giver of previously sucked boiled sweets to little children who ever was revealed to be a penguin.

'You cannot.

'Think. Who would die for a penguin, kill for a penguin, offer a penguin their money or their vote? No one. It is the place of the penguin to be as a beacon to all humanity while remaining apart, untroubled by our world and its petty affairs. You may join me in the fervent hope that our wealthy and our strong, our leaders and our led, our elected and our despots might imitate the virtues of the penguin and might wish no one to ever again die or kill or scheme or vote or suffer, or even spend a restless night on their behalf.

'So, little sisters and little brothers, so is the wisdom of my life poured out before you.'

And having spoken, the Wise Old Man glanced about him to find he had been left entirely alone. He smiled and, because he was tired at that time, settled himself to sleep beneath his particularly favourite tree. And while he dreamed, the afternoon became evening exactly as he knew it would.

FAILING TO FALL

THIS IS THE one thing I know from the minute I lift the receiver and slip that voice inside my ear – once it's there, it doesn't matter how this happens. It *will* happen.

'Come now.'
'What?'
'I need you. I need you to come right now.'
'I'm working.'
'And I'm not. I'm at home. Come on.'
'You don't – '
'I do. Tell them you're feeling ill. You've got to be somewhere. There's an emergency. This is an emergency.'
'I can't.'
'Will you come now. I want you to. I want you.'
'I can't.'
'I want you.'
'Really, it's impossible.'
But, really, it happens that way. I walk through the typing or crashing or silent corridors and clean out of the building without even noticing whether I've put on my coat. I'm on the way to somewhere else.

It seems a kind of falling and anyone can fall. When I think of it now, I wonder if we don't all wait from time to time, ready to make a dive, to find that space where we can drop unhindered. Like an internal suicide.

So I leave my work and start my fall. The door into the outside air swings snug behind me and I'm somewhere I can't go at other times. Here we all walk together; are together. Watch for our feet, see our bodies; we all of us have the same music romping inside our heads. We're moving through a big, blue waltz without a collision or a slip and I have my very own personal direction, smooth ahead of me. You could plant a wall across that direction and I would simply walk it down. Today I can do that. Look for my heart and you'll see it beating, even through my coat.

This is the only time I have when to be nothing other than me is quite enough. I love this.

It may have been raining a fortnight, there may be salted snow and litter greasing together under my feet, dog shit and vomit – the usual pavements we have to use – but today I will neither notice, nor be touched. Angels have decided it; I will be clean today. The air will shine.

And if I glance to the side, the effect is disconcerting. Things are blurred, as though I were watching them from a moving car. Once I have my direction, I can get up a fair head of speed. The final corner spirals off to my right, the sun is blazing a banner in every window and there they are, the reason I came, the taxis.

Observing this from a distance, I can't be sure why the taxis were always involved. I only know I have always taken taxis when I've been falling. When I could afford them and when I could not and when I had to borrow money before I climbed in. It was almost as if they had some claim on me. Indescribable. Sometimes I would find myself clipping that phone call short, just to get moving, to get aboard.

'Come now.'

'Yes, I'll get a taxi, I'm on my way.'

That kind of thing.

Standing there with the taxis, I pause for a wonderful moment at the stance — I enjoy that — and then I reach my hand out for the door. Inside, in the air freshener and cigarette and boot sole-smelling cab, things change. Moving away, the fear comes in.

With my face beside the window, I become acutely visible. I fill out with the feeling of being on my way and grow. It seems to me that I turn into something cinematically swollen. Surely, someone I work with, someone I know, someone representative of God's wrath will take away this much pleasure before it arrives. Because this is far too big for only me to have; I should be at work, I should be doing some intermediate something for someone I do not know. I shouldn't be growing this noticeably.

I am afraid of eyes that will see me this way and then not understand. I myself have no understanding, because

I am falling. There are meadows and opening seas of room between working and paying and shopping and cooking and eating and sleeping and general household maintenance in which I can be me, doing what I want. I no longer have to look out of the window and wonder who has my life, and if I miss it.

Seated in the expectancy of the taxi, I can love all the halts, the lights, the flaring pigeons. My journey will take forever and no time at all.

When I pay the driver I will only faintly notice how much, because money is irrelevant. It lies in my hand, defeated – just for today, we've changed places and I can pass it across with a big, careless smile before the door barks shut behind me.

There is an irregular instant when I leave the cab, a slight loss of rhythm which is no more than natural, before I push the steps away beneath me and make the slow walk to the lift. Almost there.

I plummet up the storeys in a stale little scrawled-over can with a pulse in my stomach which makes it all right. There is the flutter of arrival, of the door sliding back, the final steps, another door. Then I feel the pressure of movement between my face and another; the touch of hands, of air, of breath within breath.

And the fall is over. I know what will happen now.

I don't want to remember this. I would much rather let it be over and hope it won't come back again, but I know that I am not a strong person and that I very much miss those times when I was me and that was enough. Once every two or three months, I could change the world. I'm only human, I find that attractive, even now.

And yet on the days when I was not falling I couldn't think of it — the fall was somehow beyond my imagination. A particular sky, the movement of a breeze, a conjunction of word and feeling could give me a spasm of what I might call completeness, but for the most part I simply existed and made myself satisfied with that.

Then even that satisfaction changed, beginning at the taxi stance when I arrived one morning and found there were no cabs there, I would have to wait.

'We're out of luck.'

The voice was calm, soft, really very pleasant.

'I said we're out of luck. Odd for this time of day.'

'Yes.'

'I believe I've seen you here before.'

'That's possible.'

'I mean at this rank. I wait at this rank quite often because of what I do. It's my rank.'

'Well, I suppose it's mine, too. If it's anybody's.'

I am not normally this ill-tempered, but I was too far into my journey to focus on anything else and I never like speaking to people I don't know — it makes me feel stupid. I end up discussing the weather when the weather is all around us and both I and whoever the stranger might be must surely have noticed it. We would be better off asking each other if our faces are still there.

Against my nature and my better judgement and possibly because this was the only way that Fate could have arranged it, I turned to the stranger and asked, with a little ironic twist I was rather proud of, 'What is it that you do?'

'I beg your pardon?'

'You said you were here often because of what you do. I wondered what that was.'

'I see. What I do.' The smile was fully there now. 'I make love.'

'What?'

'That's what I do. I don't mean that's what I'm paid my wages for. I mean that's the most important thing I do. My vocation.'

I wanted to leave then — this was obviously not the kind of person I would usually speak to, not even the kind who was capable of small talk. I couldn't go, though. It was that word — vocation — I knew exactly what that meant. For a pulse or two I was aware that both of us were falling together, passing and repassing, nudging briefly as we soared down our particular trajectories. I had never before met somebody so like me. There was no need for words, but my companion spoke in any case.

'I've offended you.'

'No, no.'

'I've surprised you then. I only mentioned it

because . . . well, because I thought we had similar reasons for being here. A fling, an affair, a fuck. I'm in the right area?'

This was all delivered with a beery smirk and of course, I was alone again at once, spiralling off in a way that no one seemed able to understand. No one knew. I wanted to explain the way things were for me. What I did wasn't about sex, wasn't about running amok and dangerous diseases, perversion, sweat. At that time, I could only have said that my sole way not to feel squeezed all the time, was to set off on my little journeys to someone close whenever I needed to, no matter what. I needed to be able to fall, to meet sometimes in a way that other people didn't, to be outside the average shape of the day. Now that sounds like a whim, an eccentricity, but it was the heart of my life and a total stranger was quietly stamping all over it — purposely misinterpreting everything I was about.

I wish I had pointed that out, instead of just saying, 'No, not the same area.'

'You can tell me, it's alright. We aren't the only ones, by any means. I know the type.'

'Uh hu.'

'No, you don't see what I mean. We aren't the only ones who come here to catch taxis to do . . . things in that area. I know the look. You do, too, if you think about it. You know how it feels. You think that doesn't show?'

I didn't want to hear this. It was like watching my own reflection wink and walk away without me.

'I think something shows.'

'Naturally it shows. When I first realised — what we were all doing — when I looked at the taxis, smiling and creeping along . . . well, even now I can hardly keep from laughing.'

The people around me had stopped being together and the day looked the way it normally did. Nothing was special. There was a metallic feeling about where my liver would be and, more than anything, I felt angry.

'No, I don't understand. It's not like that.'

'Like what, exactly?'

'Like the way you make it sound — as if we all just ran about doing all that we liked. No one can do that. There are consequences, diseases, people are dying of that.'

'Pleasure isn't fatal. I've been in the same relationship for more than a decade now, we simply happen to be unconventional. I thought I'd made myself clear — this is a part of me and what I am and nobody else's hysteria will stop me from being who I am. We are careful because we care and we are happy. You have any objections to that?'

'No, no, I'm sorry.'

'Do you really not know what it's like when you want to make that call — to see him, to see her, whoever is important for you? Are you saying you'd just give it up if somebody told you to?' There was an ugly little pause. 'Surely you do that? You do call?'

'No.'

'Really?'

'I don't make calls, I just answer them.'

We didn't say anything else after that. There was a polite silence; as if something about what I said had been obscene. By the time my taxi came I didn't want it, but I took it anyway. I was going to be late and in the wrong mood and I couldn't help looking for other taxis to see who was inside and if they were happy.

That afternoon, it wasn't very good. I couldn't say what was wrong about it and we made no fuss at the time, but the atmosphere was odd. I strained somewhere in my neck.

It took several weeks before whatever difference we had developed was dispersed and for all of that time at the back of my mind there was a little fleet of taxis full of people I didn't know. They were all being special without me.

Perhaps it was that slight mental disturbance which made me keep thinking it was strange that I never made the call. I was always the one that got the taxi. Never the caller, always the called. Yet, it seemed more than likely the process could work in reverse. There was a pleasant logic in it. The only component transferred would be the element of surprise. Who would begrudge that? There would still be an expectant journey, a tension, a reward for waiting. No problem. So I made a call.

'Right now.'
 'Who is this?'
 'You know who it is. I have to see you. Come now.'
 'I can't now.'
 'I want you to.'
 'I can't.'
I waited at home for three hours and nobody came. I stayed in all that evening and nobody came.

Some time later, a matter of months, I found I was waiting at the stance for a taxi. It was going to be an innocent taxi and I felt a little embarrassed at catching it there. In fact, the whole situation was uncomfortable because I hadn't caught a taxi in hot blood since that unfortunate call and I didn't want to be doing it now. Everything was reminding me that I didn't know how to fall any more. I couldn't do it on my own.

 'Hello, I thought it was you.'
It was, unmistakably, that voice. That mouth. The steady eyes.

 'Here we are again. Not speaking?'
 'We're not here again. I'm catching a taxi because I'm late.'

 'That's a shame. Trouble at work?'
 'What do you mean?'

'Excessive absenteeism?'

I didn't have to look, I knew the mouth would be smiling.

'If it's any of your business, it was trouble at home. No more taxis. Full stop. Not needed.'

'Now that is a shame. That's terrible news. Look, I'll write this down. Call me, will you?'

'What?'

'Call me. On the telephone. That's my number.'

'Why the fuck would I do that?'

'Call me and see.'

I can only say I was shocked and, because my journey was less important than those I had been used to, I walked away without saying another word. I didn't need the stance; I could flag down a cab in the street; it didn't matter.

I don't know if you are familiar with the story of the guru who told his pupil that the meditative life was simple, as long as you never, ever, once thought of a monkey. Naturally, after this, the pupil's meditations were filled with monkeys of every colour and description, arranged in a series of faintly mocking tableaux.

I was reading to try and improve my condition of mind and I had come across this story. Every time I walked down the street I would think of the pupil, the guru, even the monkey and none of them would help me because my particular problem was the taxis. They were everywhere.

I didn't want to wonder where they were going and why. I didn't want to lie on my back in the night and hope that the phone might ring and there would be a journey and hands I could hold with my hands. I didn't want to wish for dreams of falling. But I wondered and hoped and wished almost all the time. Everything I did was something that wasn't wanted.

You can guess what came next. What else could I do but another thing I'd never intended? Who else did I know who had even the slightest experience in this field? I found I had no choice.

I hadn't thrown the stranger's number away, I had hidden it right at the back of a drawer in the hope I'd forget where I put it or that it might spontaneously combust: just disappear and go away.

I took under a minute to find it − a corner of paper torn from something more important with seven numbers printed on one side. I had a coffee and called. Engaged. The next time there was no answer; an hour later, the same. I gave the number one final try on two or three other occasions, the last of them late on a Sunday afternoon.

'Hello.'

I couldn't think what to say.

'Hello?'

We had never introduced ourselves and, even if we had, I wasn't precisely certain of what I was calling for. Perhaps help.

'I beg your pardon?'

'Hm?'

'Look, I'm going to hang up now.'

'No. I mean I – Hello.'

'Well, well, well. We met at the taxi rank, isn't that right?'

'Yes, yes, I'm sorry, we did.'

'You're sorry we did?'

'No, I'm not sorry we did, at all. I didn't mean that.'

'So why are you calling? I gave you my number for a reason – not for a casual chat. Why are you calling?'

'I . . . because I . . . am afraid.'

'Of what?'

'Of what I might do.'

'To whom?'

'I don't know. Mainly to me. I can't get this out of my head, the taxis, the journeys . . . the whole thing. I seem to have nowhere to go now. I thought, because you knew about it . . . You gave me your number.'

'Alright, alright. Don't worry. Now . . .'

I could hear a small disturbance at the other end of the line. Imagine that, the same noise, far away in a stranger's room and inside my head. Telephones are wonderful.

'Yes, here we are. Are you listening? Are you there?'

'I am, I am.'

'I want you to catch a taxi at the stance. I want you to tell it to go to the Odeon cinema. When you get there buy a ticket for the next screening in Cinema Three. Go in and take a seat in the fourth row from the back. Is that clear?'

'Yes – '

Far away in that other room, the receiver was replaced and I couldn't even say thank you, or goodbye.

And outside, the half moon risen, people were moving together again, the music was back and we were special. I stepped inside the taxi, rested my hands in my lap and let the world dip away to leave me somewhere altogether better. Even in the half dark, I knew my fingers were jumping a little with every heart beat, and we were in hot blood again.

Cinema Three was almost empty, pleasantly cool, and I tipped back my head while the trailers reeled by, feeling my breath going all the way in and then all the way out again.

'Good film, wasn't it?'

I held the receiver in both hands to stop it from shaking.

'You never came.'

'I'd already seen it.'

'I thought you would be there.'

'You thought wrong. Did you enjoy the film?'

'I . . . Well, yes, I enjoyed the film, but I was waiting for you.'

'You shouldn't have been. I didn't say I would be there. You don't know what you're calling for, do you?'

'What?'

'That's alright, I do. Give me your number at home and your number at work. Are you still there?'

'Yes.'

'Then give me the numbers. You do want this to continue, don't you?'

And, even if I had no idea what we were doing, I did want it to go on, so I passed over the numbers and that was that.

I don't think I lack pride; do you think I lack pride? In my position, you might have fed those numbers down the line and not considered it humiliating. I hadn't known why I was going to the Odeon and, yes, I had expected company, but at least something was happening now. I felt so much better, so much more special again. That isn't something you come by every day. Perhaps a month or two in the Seychelles would do it for you: a fridge full of cocaine: a night-sighted rifle and two hundred rounds. These things would be of no interest to me, but I never would blame anybody for making the best of whatever they'd got. I had a voice on the telephone.

So I do believe I kept a little of my pride, while admitting that I waited for the next call with something less than dignity. When it came, I was invited to wait by the Sunlight Cottages in the park. Call three sent me to the sea front; call four, the necropolis and on every outing, I met no one, spoke to no one, saw no one I recognised.

'I'm sorry, but what's going on?'

'Two o'clock, the Abbey. Be there.'

'But you won't be.'

'I know.'

'So why am I going?'

'Because I'm telling you to. Or don't you want to do this any more?'

'Please, I don't want to stop. I don't want that. I just want to understand what the fuck I'm doing. Please.'

There was a sigh. It came slipping all the way down miles of wire to me, soft but unmistakable.

'You still don't understand?'

'No.'

'Then there's no point in our continuing.'

'No. Please.'

I winced against the clatter of the receiver going down, but nothing happened.

'Please, don't hang up. If you explained I would understand, I'm sure of it.'

'What do you enjoy?'

'I . . . how do you mean?'

'What do you enjoy? What makes you take the taxis? What do they do to you? You must know, it's you it happens to. Your heart fists up and quivers, doesn't it? The call starts and your blood is suddenly pushed high, round your ears. You can hear it sing. There are pulses setting up all over you, ones you can't stop, and your stomach is swinging and then convulsing and then turning into a hole punched through to your back. Right?'

'Ye – '

'Right. All your senses shine – it's as if someone pulled a carrier bag off your head and life is very good and you feel special. Yes?'

'Mmm hmm.'

'And now you can remind me – did you enjoy that film?'

'Yes, I did.'

'You were there because you chose to go there – no one but you. You were happy. You were there and nowhere else, not even in your mind.'

'I think – '

'Don't think, we haven't got the time, just do it. Be there.'

'At the cinema again?'

'Do you still have my number?'

'I think so.'

'You'll find that I've changed it and I won't be ringing you again. This has already gone on too long. Good-bye.'

'No!'

'Take care of yourself. Good-bye.'

I didn't find this a very helpful conversation. I remember it very clearly, because, of course, it was the last. I imagined I might be angry, but the anger never came; there was only a numbness which would sometimes wake me in the early dawn, or lose my concentration when I worked. For a long time I thought I would just keep on that way, but the numbness faded and then I felt sad.

Particularly, I was sad because I thought I had really caught the idea of the thing. I'm not really so terribly stupid. I know about self-awareness and caring for the child within, I've read books. I figured out that it didn't matter where I was going in the taxi, as long as I went. It didn't matter who made the call. It didn't matter if there was a call, I could catch a taxi anyway, decide where I was going and then take off. I need never feel confined by my own existence again.

I took myself back to the cinema and it didn't work. I went back to the park and it didn't work. I took a taxi to cruise past that particular block of flats I had been so used to visiting and it didn't work. I walked up and down the streets, very often in the night, looking for a way into life. a tiny space to fall through, and it didn't work.

The last thing I've done is to write this. It should be that laying out all of these words and recalling the way that it felt when I really was living will help me. I've been turning the problem around here. I have even had to put myself in the place of the stranger on the telephone and that must mean we are a little closer than we were when we knew each other. Perhaps we have knowledge in common now that we didn't have then.

I can say I feel more peaceful than I have in a while and quite tired. When I read this back, it may be that things will come clearer. I think what I hope is that the sum of all I have written will amount to a tiny piece more than I intended and that piece will be what I was looking for all this time. I think that's what I hope.

ARMAGEDDON BLUE
OR
POISED ON THE BRINK
OF BECOMING A
MAGNIFICENT
SUCCESS

IT WAS NICE having time to think. Probably you could paint a Mona Lisa and knock off a novel or two in all this time you had to think. Really, it was terrific having so much time and bugger all to do, except blinking and breathing. You could suddenly get creative while you were stuck here, just bouncing out from one coast and into another.

The company even arranged for you to do nothing but the bouncing. They had tickets that only allowed you to be on the ferry, you couldn't land. You could look at the sea from the windows or from the observation deck, or you could just skip it all entirely and go straight for the dutyfree. Whole piles of novelists and poets and composers could fix up a seat in the bar, or somewhere, and not get off until they were finished creating whatever it was they were driven to create. That was pretty likely to be happening all around her, only she wouldn't know about it because she didn't know what anyone famous looked like. She didn't pay attention to people's faces.

The really big, celebrity types that she might have seen on a poster, a magazine cover, that kind of thing – a person like that would make alternative arrangements. They would all be in aeroplanes, skimming the globe, like enormous stones. That was funny, so many planes full of brains, fluttering into the clouds to get on with some retail thinking. It must affect the weather, a thing like that.

She wondered if she would make it to a brain plane. You'd know you were safe, up there – celebrity planes never crashed nowadays. There were those footballers came down one time, but they weren't really anyone. And that rugby team crashed as well, but they were only known for the accident, because after it they ate each other, all trapped up in the snow. That wasn't like getting a gold disc or an Oscar; that was just staying alive. Why should people get prizes for staying alive?

There ought to be a place where you could write and let them know, 'Look, if you're giving out awards for living then I don't intend to be pushy, but I actually very much find that my whole life is a fucking heroic struggle. On the good days, I wouldn't wish *living as me* on any kind of animal. For the bad days, I would need a whole brain plane to tell you what happens. All this shit happens. I can't describe it. I don't want to think about it. I mean, did you ever want to crack your forehead full open and lift your mind out to give it some air? That's what my life makes me want to do. So where's my prize for putting up with this?'

It would be like a big, soft walnut, your brain – there in your hands, all warm and grey. It made sense to her that the painful bits would be a slightly different colour and you could simply mark them for cutting out.

She could send the papers photographs of herself with her brain posing out there beside her. That would get them both on TV, on the chat shows. She had a definite disadvantage, not being an American, though. If you did anything like that in the States, the Yanks would give you a show of your own. You could end up with a television series or a job in politics really easily. It often crossed her mind that she should go to America.

It was good to think of America and places like that, because she was honestly still shaking after what happened at the dock. This huge noise like the biggest, deepest bell in the entire world had shattered out, completely without warning, nearly made her scream. Her position had been very calm until then – nobody had cast off, or out, which- ever direction was relevant, and the whole boat felt very solid and secure. She didn't feel she was going to plunge into certain death by drowning at any moment. She just felt as if she was standing on the roof of a little hotel.

That noise, though, it had been like Death's footstep, like a white, cold explosion inside and out. It was totally certain that when Death came walking towards her, with only her in mind, it would be with that sound. She would hear it ring from miles and days away.

When she had started to think and notice things again, she was gripping the rail at the edge of the deck, bending to face the milky water and searching for something big enough to eat a ship. She was looking for Death's smile, which sounded quite poetic but was how it had been. No one else seemed to have noticed a thing, there was no running or panic, except in her hands which would settle down fine if she kept them out of sight. She had forced herself to wonder if the white in the water had washed away from the White Cliffs. This was what you saw when you looked at a melted cliff. It was comforting to know that cliffs could be melted when she felt pretty liquid herself.

Presumably the whole deal had been to do with making the sea doors secure or some kind of stuff like that. They should warn passengers about these eventualities, because any nervous types could drop down dead, or go into a seizure about wartime experiences or torpedoes they'd seen in films. It was better to be safe than sorry with any kind of crowd, she knew that.

None of which made any difference now, because what she had to concentrate on were her legs which were about to turn unreliable. You could never be absolutely sure about when that would happen and the only way to be certain was to walk. Of course, by then it was too late. If you stepped out and the legs weren't with you, everyone knew all about it and everyone always loved to stare. That was television, for you, its influence, nobody scared to look at anything, any time – the whole of your surroundings, just entertainment.

Normally being out in the open calmed her, steadied

things up, but this was too open and too far out. Here were all of these fathers skipping aloft with the little sons perched on their backs, acting the ancient mariner and spouting shit about wind directions as if this was suddenly first and second nature. But she had taken her time and checked out the sky. That sky was not natural, not normal at all. It was a kind of Armageddon blue.

She wasn't easily frightened, she knew that. Living for three years with Robert, that meant you possibly couldn't be frightened ever again. Only there was something raw down along that horizon which would have blown Robert cleanly away and never mind her. The light was all wrong – too high and too sharp and too much. You keep your eyes on that for more than a couple of minutes and you will automatically feel the whole ship being drawn towards that edge of something and then off. You're going to slide over the edge just as smoothly as a coffin going backstage at the crematorium. And she'd seen that twice in her family, so she knew what she was talking about.

Robert knew nothing, except how to sound good. Still, he would know something new today – that when she said good-bye, she meant it. He could do what he wanted now with anyone he liked and it would be entirely no concern of hers. He would also be doing it without his pills, because she had them. Before she got on to the boat she'd taken one blue, two brown and four red and yellow. The two brown were for motion sickness, but the rest were his and doing a very good job against Robert sickness. It would mean that she had to go a bit carefully with the drink, but that was easily done. Anyway, they gave out these rules and recommendations for people with lousy constitutions who couldn't mix and match, but she had an excellent constitution.

Without Robert she was an excellent person. Everyone had been right, he was a manipulator and *her* departure was long overdue. This was a man who called her names, but admitted to shooting cats. He said it would alter his karma and mean he had to be reincarnated as a cat which he would prefer over anything else. One huge lie, of course. He didn't like cats and he was a psycho, that was all.

Celibacy was the only way and was very fashionable now. If she had been celibate all the while she wouldn't have met up with Billy who got depressed, or Ian who had the snakes, or Mark who was so like her father it made her feel sick, even to imagine the shape of his head from the back, and none of that shit would have happened. She must qualify for an award on the strength of Mark alone, never mind all three.

She would be celibate until really the correct person for her made himself obvious and then start out properly. They would have nice children and no reptiles or guns, not even little ones.

Until then, she would have a holiday. In Europe for a little while she would get brown skin and blonde hair on her arms. She was going to learn how to bicycle and relax. There would be wine and happiness, clean dust in the streets and it was only a matter of time before she discovered something she was very good at and became a magnificent success.

BRACING UP

He shouldn't sleep on his back, you know, really he shouldn't. Only caused trouble. He didn't know why he had tonight — that was last night now, because this was the morning. He hadn't even dozed on his back in years, not since he woke up choking one time, dreaming that he was drowning and finding out almost too late that he was right. You forgot these previous incidents and then there was trouble, guaranteed.

Not to mention all that nonsense the Victorians worried about; sewing corks at the back of the nightshirt, preventative ropes knotted round the pyjamas, night-time boxing gloves. Must have been generations of boys who grew up masturbating on their sides — little Sons Of Empire rounding their shoulders for life.

God, that was it, you see, thinking rubbish like that. Sleep on your back and your head silts up.

And if there were any fairness in the world, this morning he should really be clear-headed, even pleased. Before she left, he remembered, he asked her to do three things, the three things he'd always wanted someone else to do so that he could go back to sleep again after and wake up to find them still there. Done. In many ways that was better than waking to find *her* still there, Much more convenient.

'I'm sorry?'

'Oh, just three things, if you could do them for me. Nothing odd. I promise.'

'Well, I suppose that's a relief.'

She'd laughed then, uncomfortably, because he was making her uncomfortable – not on purpose, he just was uneasy to be with sometimes, he knew that.

'You are going to get up and show me out, though, aren't you? I don't even think I remember the way I came in. And I'd rather not – '

'Meet anybody. No, you wouldn't want to meet them. They're all arseholes, as it happens, but you wouldn't want to meet them anyway.'

'They did very well, last night, though. It was a good show. I've always liked "Lear". What's wrong?'

'Nothing. But we needn't talk about that, need we. You have to leave. Before they all wake up. And there were those three things, before you go, if you didn't mind.'

He thought of her leaving, of what she would see. She would remember him standing in the big, wooden doorway, bare feet out on the stone of the landing, numbed. She would see him pale, skin almost as white as his crumpled boxer shorts, his bagging T-shirt and the stairwell still dim, but all of him very obviously yellowed over by the dirty skylight. Bullet head, barrel chest, arms too close to some kind of breaking-point. And his legs were awful. He would look along his legs in the bath, right down to the deathly blueness of his feet and there could be a tag there, tied to one of his toes with a name and address, cause of death. Wouldn't seem out of place. Dead legs and desperate arms — he looked like the boxer you knew would lose the fight.

Before he got out of bed and disgusted her completely, he should have her do those things.

'I do promise I'll see you out. All I'm doing is keeping warm. You can understand that.'

'Warm? This is Paris out there, remember? You don't need to keep warm.'

'I've been here for a while and now it's autumn. I'm feeling the cold.'

He pressed his fingertips up to his forehead, as if he might be thinking. He couldn't feel a sweat, so she wouldn't see one. Besides, it wasn't hot yet, only warm, he would be able to feign coldness fairly convincingly.

'Could you draw back the curtains?'

'Is that one of your things?'

'Yes it is. It's the first.'

'Fine. That OK?'

'Lovely.'

He winced while light something like a sheet of milky blue water fell over the bed clothes and his head. Barely past dawn, then. Her hair was more red than he'd thought. When the light shone through it like that, it became extremely red.

'Lovely. I enjoy watching the mornings here. They're such a lazy colour of blue. Precise and extravagant but very lazy. Do you know what I mean?'

'I don't John, but then I'm quite tired. I think I have a hangover, don't you?'

'Me? Not really.'

But then he hadn't drunk as much as her. That was the whole point; you should seem to be drinking and very loud and easy and they really did drink and then eventually they would do what you suggested – accompany you home. Sometimes. He hadn't thought it would work here – too unsophisticated. You might imagine that in Paris you would have to be sophisticated. Then again, she was English and not sophisticated at all.

'I don't often get hangovers. Open the window, please.'

'You are a funny man, John. It was John, wasn't it?'

'Yes.'

He had to say that quickly or the atmosphere would go. He didn't want the whole scene turning cheap on him, not now.

'Won't the draught make you cold?'

'No. It will make me relaxed. It feels blue when you breathe it inside, calming, the morning air, hadn't you noticed? With you being a new arrival, I thought . . .'

He was losing this, he could tell by her eyes, although

actually, she was still a little smashed. Either that or just clumsy, but he hadn't noticed her being clumsy before. He cleared his throat before the complicated bit.

'And now, do you have anything . . . that is . . . Yes, there's a little tin of sweets in my jacket pocket.'

'I know, I bought one too.'

'Mm. But you opened yours and I didn't open mine and so we should swap.'

'What?'

'Swap. There are different cats on the tins, too, did you notice? I buy them a lot and I think there are five types of cat. The one I have would suit you better. And you'd get a full tin.'

Don't push it.

'They're strawberry. Very nice.'

'I know, I opened my tin, remember?'

'Fraise de Bois – I know you know – the woman in the shop, not the one you saw, her mother, she used to pick them where she lived. In the woods – near the woods – wild strawberries. That must have been nice, she always smiles when she talks about it. She says there were *sangliers*, too – wild boars – which I don't believe for a moment.'

Shut up. Shut up. She is very clearly beginning to be alarmed.

'Can we swap, then? Please.'

'Is that it, John?'

'Mm?'

'Number three?'

'Oh, yes. Yes it is.'

She walked to his jacket with her tin. Did she hesitate before reaching into his pocket? Did she seem a touch disgusted by contact with it? Wrong side. It was the right-hand side she wanted. Yes — his cat out and her cat in. He could make a joke about that but he wouldn't because there would be no point. You could hear the small rattle of the sweets and watch her dip down her hands, as if they were going into water. The woman had very smooth hands.

'Thank you.'

'For what? Now I've got more than you.'

'Doesn't matter, I can buy more if I want to. Turn your back.'

'What for?'

'Because I'm getting out of bed.'

'No. Don't be ridiculous.'

So she would see him now — all of him — and that would be that.

Lost it. Lost it. Lost it.

And she had such a nice cunt.

He'd gone back to bed once she'd left, the soles of his feet still burning against the sheets after the chill of the stone. And yes, now he remembered, he'd lain on his back to look at the sky through the window, must have dozed back off without ever moving.

The sun was strong in his eyes now and the street smell

drifting in was hot, dust in it and a little bit of something cooking. There was Middle Eastern dance music from across the road again and down by the river one of those tinny, bloody engines was passing — sounded more like a sewing-machine than a car. Or it could be a scooter. Either way, it was an ugly sound to be out in such a lovely sky.

The place must have been much quieter during the war when they had the taxi bicycles and bugger all else. Only then there would have been sirens and Vichy cars full of Nazi petrol, the odd bit of gunfire, screaming resistants.

It was so hard to imagine all this being occupied. Christ knew, there were plaques all over the walls to remind you of this or that hero *Tombé Pour La Patrie*. It made you wonder who it was remembered all of that falling so accurately until after the war. And then forgot they shouldn't like fascists. But of course, Europe was like that — terribly forgetful. Why else would it be so good at wars?

Impossible, when you thought about it, to believe anything had ever happened here — the war, the Nazis, he found it all beyond him. The sky was too relaxing and the statues were too golden, up in the blue, and probably he was just too far from home to care, no recent invasions of his own to compare theirs with.

The sweets would be there in his jacket pocket. That was good, something from someone else's handbag and someone else's hands inside his own pocket, right in there.

He could stare through the curtains that someone else had opened and think about that.

The others would wake up soon, so he would have to take his bath and get out of the way. He could do with being really clean, down to the skin, that kind of clean. For instance, he could feel the stubble coming on his arms.

She'd asked about that, hadn't she? Not shy – drunk, really, but she wouldn't be shy sober, you could tell that.

'You've got no hair.'

'I beg your pardon?'

'Turn on the light, you've got no hair.'

She would laugh at him. This would be the place where she would laugh at him, wouldn't it?

He took one of her hands by the wrist, rather firmly and pressed it against his cheek.

'I have hair.'

'Alright, OK, OK. I can feel it, I saw, but you don't, I mean there should be – '

'Listen!'

That was too loud. He felt her jump against him, knew the others might have heard. He should let go of her wrist and pat the back of her hand, let his fingers slide to her shoulder as if this was all very natural for him.

'Listen. Sorry. Sorry, but I do know what I'm talking about, you see? I do know me rather better than you do and we are talking about me and I have hair on my head and my face like bristles on a bloody pig, but I don't have

any hair anywhere else. Anywhere else. No need to look
— that's how I am.'

'Hey, I'm . . . it doesn't worry me. It's alright.'

'Why should you worry about it? I don't worry about
it.'

'But were you born like that? Did something happen?'

Jesus Christ, he wanted to punch her. He just wanted
to punch her and she didn't even know, she wouldn't be
in the least expecting it if he did. Stupid, stupid woman.
The joke was on him, of course, she wouldn't be here if
she wasn't stupid.

'No, I wasn't born like this. But I am like this now.
OK? Satisfied?'

'I am. Please forget about it. It's only unusual, that's
all.'

'Well, so am I.'

Which made her laugh in he thought a nice way. Sur-
prising, that.

Trouble was, he'd forgotten, which was not unlikely,
quite to be expected, really. He'd forgotten that most
people don't do that. They don't take off their hair and
get that really clean feeling as if their skin was thinner and
everything was that tiny bit closer; the touch of cloth so
fresh. Other people didn't slip into bed and feel so incred-
ibly near the sheets. Or if they did, they hadn't told him,
which was another problem in itself. Fucking generally
unfriendly people round here — all dark glasses and yappy
little dogs. Even in the rain, even at night, for Christ's

sake, there were leashes and rat-headed dogs and those blacked-out eyes, looking straight at you but not letting on. He'd bought some shades himself – look local and all that.

He would get himself ready now, clean out the bath and be away before he had to speak to any of them: Annie and Pat, practically bloody children he was working with here, and that prick Robbins: cocky bastard. And nothing to be cocky about – seen fish with a better grasp of rhythm. Spoke the verse as if he was coughing up blood, but he was sly, you could see he was sly and that would get him forward.

'Thank you for that, Mr Hughes. I'm learning a lot.'

Blood sucking little prick. Go on stage and you could feel him, licking up every move, every pause for breath, and stowing it away. Vampire. And why be so fucking polite? He'd had the proper training, the accredited drama school and the nice grant, he'd make it, there was no question. He was a pretty boy and he would make it. Why not just say it, right out – here I am, half your age, playing your part, the one you'll never get and I don't even have the fucking grace to care.

But he wouldn't say anything like that because, as you knew, he was bloody sly.

'Mr Hughes?'

'John.'

'Thank you, I don't feel too comfortable with first names. I can be shy. I noticed, John, you made a change there, tonight.'

'What do you mean?'

'In the prophecy, you put in, well, I don't know what I would call it. You didn't change the sense, but you put in a syncopation, didn't you. It made all the difference.'

'I didn't notice, I just open my mouth and the words come out. No training, you see, so no tricks.'

Not that I'm telling you, anyway, boy. Not that I'm telling you. 'Made all the difference'. Implication being, it was bloody awful before. I know you Jim Robbins, inside and out. Been there.

Yes, better to get up and out and save all the good morning smiles and 'Can we get you a lovely fresh croissant while we're out; such a nice bakery and only across the street, that's Paris for you. And Annie has more of her wonderful jam.' Poor cow, she looked like a sack of cement already and still going heavy on the jam. She'd spend the rest of her life doing bits as comedy feminists and dykes which was a shame because, fair play, she was good. Apart from her size.

Yes, up and out would be the better choice – avoid hellos and awkwardness.

Funny that he still had such a clear image of that woman's face and the shape her curled legs made under the sheet. Walking down the sand yellow steps to the embankment and the river he tried to make himself still inside, to let her ease away. After all, he wouldn't see her again.

It was too early for the sun to get into the stone, but

the wall behind him, the fat block under him where he sat, were beginning to flare with light. The coolness from the river was pushing up under his chin and feet and the sun was pressing down. His hair was drying – he liked to let it do that in the sun, the process seemed to make the bristle finer. He could smell his own aftershave, soap, a trace of depilatory cream, the laundering and cloth in his shirt. Everything to do with him smelt clean.

Back up on the street, away from the surprisingly sweet river, there must be a Métro station because there were snatches of that, too – a very warm, very dry, almost spiced kind of smell. It was hard to pin down, but exactly the smell of the Métro and nothing else.

He reached into his pocket for the sweet tin and pulled off the sharp metal lid with its black and white cat. Here they even drew their cats to look foreign: that was to say, French. He could almost feel the scent of imitated strawberry and sugar. It made him twitch his nose. The cotton of his trousers was snug over his legs, smooth, his shoes giving out a good shine. In fact, he couldn't deny that he was well turned out in an exterior way. She was still there inside, though, with that sickly way of smiling and her short nails. If she gave him a hard-on now that would not be neat.

The soil here was ridiculous, like face powder or crumbled biscuit with shells of flint. He adjusted the weight on his shoulders and began to enjoy the easiness in his walk.

Brace up, John, brace up.

He didn't need to do this, of course, the show was paying him enough, he didn't need to work the booth, might have left it at home instead of dragging it round like a bloody penance.

He couldn't have left it, though. He couldn't have come here and stayed for so many months knowing that he hadn't the choice just to walk away one morning and set up the booth, get inside the guts of it where no one else could join him, because no one else would fit.

The booth always gave him the feeling he had when he sat absolutely still in the middle of very loud music; just didn't move anywhere, but in his head. Used to make his grandfather demented, that.

'Why don't you bloody breathe, boy. Sitting there, like you were stuffed. Enjoy yourself; everyone is looking.'

But he would keep on sitting, knowing that he would certainly one day completely explode with the pressure of music and secrets and hate packed up inside him. He would try to imagine his grandfather's face when that happened – when John Boyce Hughes suddenly burst into powder and fire.

But now he was going to put down the booth and grow; that was how it worked. Before he did anything else, he would just stand with that weight lifted off and feel his legs, his neck, his back, all easing upwards and a little over scale.

'Brace up, John, brace up.'

That was very nice, to brace up like that, nobody needed any more to tell you that you should be taller or straighter or bigger than you were, because you knew all about it. No need for grandfathers now, the job was done.

Which didn't mean you wouldn't hear those words, fumbling about in the back of your mind, and in *his* voice, mind you, not even your own bloody voice. You would hear him from all of those times before, you would see the words dripping down from under that old yellow rag of a moustache.

'Brace up, John. Brace up.'

That awful operatic rumble he had, down under the wheezy lungs and the tar. God, you could really almost actually see him, hunched under one of those slim little trees over there, slapping his hands down hard on the black hoop armrests of his chair. Horrible old chair, like something he'd made up out of his head. He would sit under the silver green leaves and whatever you did, you would feel him looking at you and then through and out at the back, like always.

'How did you do at school, then? Still stupid?'

'I don't, I don't know.'

'Ha! So what does that make you? Not even knowing. Ha!'

'Stupid. Stupid, *Tad-cu.*'

'What?'

'Stupid, *Tad-cu.*'

'Which means.'

'Hn?'

Because you couldn't say a word then. He knocked all the words clear out of you, you see, not laying a finger anywhere near you, but hurting and making it not possible to speak, because he was looking at you, because he was there. And probably he wasn't even concentrating so terribly much on you, you not being so terribly important. He would be speaking, but also rolling up a thread of cigarette, tight as his mind.

'*Tad-cu*: it means? Surely to God, you haven't forgotten.'

'Grandfather. It means grandfather, grandfather.'

Words getting slippery with panic. Very hard to get out in the open air. You seemed to squeal instead of speaking.

'Literal translation.'

'Gra- Um . . . Father. Dear father. Kind father.'

And he would bloody wait. You knew you'd got it right, absolutely, but he couldn't, he wouldn't say. He would just stare you out; see if he could push you to change your mind, to cry, to do anything other than stare at him back and try not to swallow again and not to blink.

John thought of the smile shining under his grandfather's moustache, a flicker of something hard and slick, before another drift of smoke rolled up and hid it away.

'So, I'm your dear father, am I?'

'Yes.'

'Don't yelp. You're a boy, not a dog. A boy with Welsh

blood in him and we'll make a Welsh man of you, will we not? Even if you were born out of place. Dudley. Dudley, I ask you, why the bloody hell your mother ever came here and ruined herself . . . Ruined you. Didn't think of that, though, did she, spoiling her own son.'

It was nice, being spoiled, you knew what you were and where you were immediately and forever. Many people never had something like that.

John dropped the pins into the hinges carefully, feeling his Tad-cu still watching, like a smoky blurr from under the tree. Still, never mind the old bastard, the booth was taking shape now and becoming the small miracle it was designed to be. He had made it a box that could hold him completely, or fold up and fit on his back. People would come up to watch only that. Children who couldn't stay long enough to see the show would stand and see the panels turned upward and outward, high and smooth in solid crimson and gold.

But nobody saw the best bit, nobody came with him inside into the black brown canvassy dark that pressed his skin to the bone. It smelt of him in here: cloth, sweat, earth, skin: himself.

Hook the puppets up under their shelf, being both gentle and precise, letting the feathers settle, things like that. You check the curtains and let your mind flow through what it will do today, nice and easy, no sweat, yet. Then stop altogether, take a breath, get full of breath. Ready.

'Hello, God.'

Lovely. It always made him laugh to say that. Even the first time.

'Go up any hill in Wales, boy, and you can talk to God. They're all Mount Sinai, they're all Ararat. We have them so we can be closer to God. You understand?'

'Yes, Tad-cu, I do understand.'

'Then look it, John Hughes, look as if you bloody understand.'

And they'd gone, of course. Only the once, but they'd gone to Wales, away from that sulphur and metal Midland air and into something else. It was somewhere in the North, they stayed – up above a little horseshoe bay and a village Tad-cu wouldn't say if he knew or not. No one seemed to know him, but that might have been because of his moustache which perhaps he hadn't had before.

Didn't matter, anyway, not at all, because up above the village, there was space to run away. You were encouraged to run away. There was an entire hill there, almost a mountain, for you to climb up and make yourself fit and manly and Welsh.

The heat in the booth, it always reminded you of lying down flat on the banks that hid the pathway when it turned above the tree line. You would wait there for the crickets to sing.

At first, you couldn't find them and then as soon as they heard you running, they would stop, as if they'd been something you'd only had inside your mind. But then you learned to be still and to wait and those high pulsing notes would start up in the wiry grass, all around you, perhaps because they had forgotten you, or perhaps because you were no longer frightening. Their noise had frightened you at first, when it was so close and surrounding. Then you learned to see them, with the tiny stripes of different green along their sides and the pink, too, an amazing kind of pink. They looked wonderful, like God's little singing machines.

He stayed with the crickets for hours, not really wanting to go any higher, in case God saw him. Only there seemed to be nothing up there, if you looked, except some sheep and hillocky grass, rabbits maybe. So, in the end, it seemed safe to edge towards the top of the hill, a touch more each time.

At one point, you could shield your eyes from the sun, the way explorers did and overlook the next valley. There were villages pressed into its curve, like cups lined with scales of slate. Everywhere there were people here, there was slate: tiles and slabs and big, ragged teeth of it, speared down into the ground for fences. Slate and smoke and people and slate – this must be the way God saw it, rings of smokey slate, way down under, anchoring threads of prayer.

On the second last day they spent there, John walked really to the summit. He could remember himself some days, even in the booth, lowering to his knees and sinking into the comfortable spring of turf, up high, up there.

He'd kept his eyes looking ahead while he filled his lungs taut against his stomach and chest. There were other hills, higher than his where God would very likely be close enough to make something fire and cloudy happen – scare hell out of the poor bugger sheep – but this was as far as he could risk.

He battened down his thoughts and fed out the words, high as those further hills. Must have been as high as that, perhaps more.

'Hello, God.'

He'd thought he would die, be called up to the angels and away from his spoiling and from Tad-cu and his high black chair. Didn't happen, of course.

In the end he was so scared, so sprung with waiting for blazing wings to lift him off that he couldn't do anything but run and when he fell, he rolled and scrambled and ran even more, making his ears pop, he was dropping so fast and not even minding the eyes of the clever ram licking over him as he passed.

After a while, it seemed good that God didn't want him yet. It was just bad that Tad-cu still did.

There were people outside now, children. He could watch them through the gauze, see what they were like, how best to please them.

He worked Pool on to his arm, took the wing rods and smoothed the feathers perfect. No crow had ever had feathers like this. He knew that because he had made them, his creation. They seemed to live and so did Pool the crow, because John knew how to do that, the timing, the manipulation, like clockwork silk. He knew about puppets. He pushed his face nearer the gauze.

'Want me to make you happy, then? Lucky little bastards. Lucky little French bastards. All the same really though, aren't you? Just want to be happy. I know.'

That woman, she could have come in here with him, the first time anyone else had done that. There would have been barely room for them both; they would have had to stand very close. It would be like bringing somebody into his home, his real home.

Not that you brought it along — the booth — because you were some kind of snail. Perfectly possible to be at home anywhere. No, this was a reminder to the others that he could do something they could not. It was a confidence thing, worked both ways, helped him up and left them down. Everyone knew that only he could do puppets — the moves, the voices — never mind walking into 'Lear' with Pool on his arm, being the Fool and being the bird, swapping the lines between them as if he was born expressly to do nothing other than that and making it different every night. You couldn't say that wasn't good, wasn't more than alright.

Pool would look at Mr Robbins tonight and sing.

He that has and a little tiny wit,
With heigh-ho, the wind and the rain,
Must make content with his fortunes fit,
Though the rain it raineth every day.

Pool could have all that, because it left John his face
free to watch with and then to say the prophecy which
was more fun. Things like that, he could choose how he
did them and the others could not, ask all the questions
they liked.

'Mr Hughes, John, tell me, how do you see the Fool?'

'Mr Robbins, all the Fool does is to tell you that you're
stupid and all that you do is to prove that he is right.'

'Ha, that's good, John. That's awfully good.'

'Don't mention it, Jim.'

While he packed down the booth again, finished up, he
could feel the two boys watching. They smiled when he
looked at them. He smiled back.

'Gentlemen, if you don't go away, I am entirely likely
to beat your little heads in. Now fuck off, fun's all over.'

The boys kept on smiling, eyes slightly clouded,
but the mother came and scooped them off. Must have
understood. Most people did, You tried to return the
compliment — swap languages the way they all seemed
to, but sometimes. Well, sometimes. That girl in the
office, every day, the exact same thing.

'Bon matin, Monsieur Hughes.'

But how did she pronounce it? YooGess. Like that, YooGess.

He'd told her and she hadn't listened, or something hadn't clicked because she kept on saying, 'YooGess'.

'No, no. Look. *S'il vous plaît. Soyez vous si gentille d'écouter.* Hn? Hn?'

Little expectant face she turned up to you at that point.

'The last time I say this. *La dernière fois.* OK?'

'OK.'

'Hughes. *Mon nom est Hughes. Après moi. Um . . . comme la chanson* "Harley Davidson". That song. *Vous la connaissez?* Well, I'm not going to bloody sing it. "*Je ne connais plus personne, en* Harley Davidson." Hn? *Huh.* OK?'

'OK.'

'OK. Fine. Then . . . *puis* . . . Oooo. *Comme 'il est où?'* Ooo. OK? *Huh* – Ooo. *Puis* . . . *Puis*, Zzz. *Comme les mouches,* eh? Zzz. *Huh* – oo – zzz.'

'*Oui, YooGess.*'

'*Non! Encore une fois!*'

Embarrassing in the end because she was crying and the manager seemed to think it was all because she was black. Hadn't even noticed she was black, nothing to do with it, she had no pronunciation – that was all. The whole thing had been messy – the sort of confusion you could only get in a cheapskate little theatre, up the arse end of an impasse.

Girl hadn't spoken to him since and she'd flicked him a

nasty smile when he left with that woman; with, Martha.
Fuck, that was her name, God help us, she was called
Martha, he'd remembered. Astonishing. He could
imagine Tad-cu's face at that.

'Martha boy, Martha, what kind of a bloody name is
that, then? English, is she? With you, is she? There's a
bloody miracle. Ha!'

But she was English and she was with him – had been
with him. Martha had been with him all night and, in a
way, he could thank Tad-cu for it – all those Welshness
lessons to fit all her neat little questions.

'Where are you from, John?'

'Hm?'

'Where are you from? You have an accent I can't place.'

'Oh, I've moved so much, you see. There's hardly
anything left.'

But you should paste it on thick now, Boy Bach, otherwise this will not work.

'I'm . . . well, I'm Welsh, really.'

'Really?'

'Yes.'

'Where?'

'The North. You wouldn't know it, only small, see –
the place. The crow – you know the crow I have in the
play?'

'I loved it.'

'Thank you. The crow is called Pool, but actually it's
Pwyll – after Pwyll, Prince of Dyfed.'

'Say that again.'

Oh, the lure of a foreign language.

'Pwyll.'

Got her. You should smile now, big and shy, let the hands fold on to the table. She would like to look at the size of your hands. There's lovely, but never as lovely as now, and look in her eyes.

'Who was — ?'

'Pwyll? He was a mythical hero — only kind we have. My grandfather taught me about him, taught me lots of things like that. He brought me up. My mother and father . . . they weren't around.'

'That's awful.'

Yes, it bloody was, but not tonight. Tonight it is only useful.

'No, not awful, not really. Hard sometimes, that's all.'

But everything serves a purpose eventually — even Tad-cu — all you have to do is wait.

Martha proved that was right. After the show, she'd been almost grateful. She shook your hand. No, she shook your wrist; held you there, very firmly and smiled full in your face.

'You were wonderful. Why didn't you take your bow?'

'Oh I . . . My part is over so long before the end. Sometimes I even leave the building. It's um . . . I'm glad you liked it.'

And you were glad. You could let in her liking and be glad because she couldn't harm you. You'd waited so long that no one could harm you again. You had been patient and certain that people would like what you did in the end and wouldn't hurt you. You just had to wait.

Even Tad-cu, he couldn't reach you now. He'd pushed you so far inside – done it himself – that he couldn't get you and now it was safe to come out and take what you'd always been waiting for.

Not like the first time, the first time wasn't fair. When you're still young you never know what to expect, you don't know what might be reasonable, what might not. Like the first show you did, the first thing half worth looking at and a sort of party going on this one night – somebody's birthday. You'd known Tad-cu had been out there watching, nice seat, but he hadn't come round – not a sign of him.

In the end, you'd gone out to see what was up and there the old bastard was, out in the alley. He made you wait while he clamped out his cigarette on the brickwork, spat and wiped his mouth. And you started to shiver. The grease and the sweat and the scrubbing were starting to chill you through while he stood there, wiping his fucking mouth and making you speak.

'Well? What did you think?'

'Well, John.'

Slow walking, the slithery kind of grind his boots made on the dirty street.

'You are John Hughes, aren't you?'

'Hh? I, I . . . Tad-cu?'

'Oh, yes, I recognise you, now you're stuttering again.'

Then his fist smoothing into your face along the length of those words, as if it was a part of them. And you going down on the pavement and hearing him keep on talking while you tried to breathe and felt the warm stuff on your face, that drowning feeling making it clear that your nose was broken — that bad feeling — even worse because you were almost sure he was going to kick you now.

'Spoiled. I said you were spoiled and I was right. No one with our name will ever do what you just did. No one. What was it supposed to be? Ha?'

And you'd thought he would like it. For no good reason, but you'd thought it might be something he'd be proud of. You'd been doing a Welshman, for Christsake. Bloody convincingly, too.

'Never seen anything like it. Never heard anything like it. My own flesh, my grandson, an Uncle Tom, a creature who would sell his own country. And for what? Ha? For what?'

You flinching as the boots walk away, ashamed of being afraid again and almost angry enough to be unafraid, only now you feel sick.

The doorman's face as you make your way in again, blood on your shirt.

Strange how people assume you will be unable to perform with a broken nose. Strange how they let you go with a sympathetic smile, because you are spoiled and they cannot wait to see that you'll get better. Generally impatient lot in the theatre, immune to reason, unable to understand what a man like that might do to you.

But you beat him in the end — the man who scared you right off the stage, pushed your whole personality into a bundle of cloth and wires at the end of your arm and slapped you in a booth almost for life. The one who made sure you were spoiled before you were even as old as Robbins, or Annie, or Pat. You beat him, didn't you? Yes you did. You waited and you did.

God knew, you hadn't even seen Dudley, not for twenty years, more, and suddenly you felt safe to go back there. Something had lifted from you and it would be safe, you knew, he couldn't hurt you now.

He wasn't in the house. The house, the street it stood in, that whole district had been removed. It made you feel slightly less real, yourself, losing something like that.

You walked about between the blocks of new, metal factory units and the nicely curved roads with grass verges and the men in overalls, sitting out to eat their lunch, even in that thick, slightly bitter air. Funny how the air didn't change, even if the industries had, even if you had.

He wasn't there.

He didn't seem to be anywhere except inside your nights with the old dreams and sour air. You had almost begun to relax, to walk the town as if you were allowed there when you thought to check the hospitals and the homes. He might be hiding, still alive.

And you found him. In Ethelfleda House – big Viking influence at work here, you see. Oddly warped sense of history they had, like naming boulevards after Goebbels, but then, why not. Nobody really cared any more, after all, and now there were Viking shopping malls, playparks named after the heathen invaders, all very civilised. Like Ethelfleda House – that was very civilised, too – it presented no problems, not one difficulty. You walked into his room without anyone doing anything other than smiling and nodding hello. It would be possible to stroll by, any time – throttle the life clean from him and skip out again before anyone knew a thing.

'Hello there.'

'Who are you?'

'Who am I? I thought you might know.'

'Good God.'

'Isn't he? Brought me here. Aren't you going to say you're glad to see me?'

'No, I'm not. You can go now, John Hughes. Get out and go.'

'But I've only just got here. I've only just begun to see what a pitiful bloody place this is you've landed in. Been here long, have you? Expect to get out again? Ever? Feet first job, won't it be? Eh, Tad-cu?'

'Bugger off.'

Arrogance never wore off, did it? Maybe because it

never did have much to do with reality, capability, only to do with belief — fear and belief, like God.

'I'll bugger off in my own good time, thank you. Bury you round here, will they? Far away from the green, green grass of home Dear me. Where was it you came from? I don't remember. You were always too busy making me Welsh to say.'

'I have a button. I can push it and they'll come '

So you take his sodding button on its sodding cord and possibly give him a tap on the head, a small knock to get his attention, brace him up.

'You little bastard. You always were a little bastard. A bastard.'

'Shut up and stay shut up or I will kill you. I swear, I'll kill you now. For once in your life, listen to me. I'm moving back home. I'm going to come and see you, every day. You're on the ground floor here. I could come and watch you in the night — terrible locks, you have here — anyone could climb in and do anything while you slept. Do you sleep well? And did you miss me? I'm the only family you've got. Did you miss me, while I was away?'

Well, naturally, it was upsetting — him starting to shake, to whimper. Eventually, you stopped speaking because he obviously couldn't hear you. Not paying attention in any way. He was just blubbing like anything and shaking his head — odd.

And you had this perverse desire to pat his clawed-up,

sepia-stained hand where he'd left it on the arm of the chair – not his old chair, something much more institutional. Nothing of his own furniture seemed to be there, hardly anything personal at all. You didn't touch him, though, no time left for that.

'Tad-cu? Tad-cu, before I go I'd just like to say you're a poor lonely bugger and you'll stay that way. And in the end, there'll only be me to carry your memory and you know what I'll do with it, don't you? So ta-ta. Nos da, in fact, eh? Nos da.'

He couldn't even meet your eyes.

Had no intention of seeing him again – on a train within the hour and never been back. Never will be back. Enough to know he could be beaten and that all of it was over with, finished.

Something else to tell Martha, there, of course.

'Oh, he was taken into care. My work, you see. I couldn't look after him properly. Well, we separated in a way – didn't get on – and he died there. In care. In England – buried there, too, which he wouldn't have liked.'

'I'm sorry.'

'Thanks. Have some more of this. I have a terrible head for drink. Never know what I'll do. You want to finish the bottle?'

Would she come and see the show again? See him again?

Ridiculous question. When had there ever been anyone came back for more?

Best thing all round would be to go home to the apart-
ment and have a bath because the sweat would half blind
you in that booth and you didn't want to walk about
unclean that way. Better to sweat the dirt out and then
scrub clean, the way the Romans did.

He walked to the theatre, like always, it wasn't far and
the evenings were good. He could cool his mind and
straighten his limbs, get ready to be there.

'Here we are again then, God. Off to play the Fool,
same as ever. It's all the same game, though, anyway,
isn't it? You and me, thinking things up and then making
them alive. No disrespect, it's a nice game, thank you.
You know, I wish it could have been the other way,
though. Two more weeks and this will be over, back to
the booth and nothing but the booth, and I was hoping
for something else because I did alright here, didn't I? I
did alright. People said so. They said I made the show. It
isn't fair, you see, getting a taste of something and then
never being able to do it again. For that to happen twice
in one life-time, that isn't fair, is it, God?'

There was a pleasant softness to the sky – birds coming
down for the evening, little sparrows. A party of men in
red hats was taking photographs – a broad huddle of
smiles against another good skyline, this time with a
golden angel and a bridge.

'Maybe if I'd spoken to you from a higher hill. You
remember that time? Would you have heard me then? If

I'd made the effort to get that bit further up, would you have listened?

'Because I didn't get what I asked for, not really, and I do wonder why. Not that there's any point knowing now, it's just that I wonder. You understand?'

THE MOUSEBOKS FAMILY DICTIONARY

THE EXTRACT FROM the Mouseboks Family Dictionary which follows is compiled and freely given to the world by Francis L. Mouseboks XIIc 'That the name of Mouseboks may resound with every dawning in all its manifold glory and delight.'

anticipation: All Mousebokses spend their lives in a constant condition of *Anticipation*, principally of their own or other's deaths. As *Anticipation* of their own demise maintains them perpetually on the brink of *Despair* while the idea of anyone else's dying makes their lives extremely pleasing, if not actually worthwhile, Mousebokses may appear to be of rather changeable temperament.

Prolonged financial, sexual or fearful *Anticipation* is almost always fatal in Mousebokses. This means that all Mousebokses do effectively die of *Anticipation*, thus vindicating any morbid *Anticipations* they might have harboured of their own deaths. As all Mousebokses are painfully aware of this family weakness, each and every Mouseboks Family Member is inwardly contorted by strenuous efforts to avoid anticipating even the slightest

Anticipation of an *Anticipation* and so on into a thankfully early grave.

Even very brief *Anticipation* is certainly always fatal to those inducing it in Mousebokses. See *Money*, *Murder*, *Sex*, *Lust*, *Fear of Psychiatrists*, and *What you Deserve*.

arms: The Mouseboks Family has no particular coat of arms, although all their coats do, naturally, have arms. Unless they are waistcoats, as not worn by Mouseboks Family *Uncles/Cousins/Brothers*. Also Mouseboks Family members dream very frequently of bearing arms, most often against other Mouseboks Family members.

aunt (old):   Like a Savings bank, but more mobile and whimsical.

aunt (young):   See *Lust*.

bad joke: See *Life*.

Or *Bad Jokes* are frequently told by Mousebokses at times of extreme stress/family gatherings etc. Comic effect marred only by Mousebokses' inability to concentrate on human beings beyond themselves, or to remember punchlines.

birth: Whether as onlooker or active participant, something any Mouseboks will always deeply regret. Note all

Mousebokses have marked aversion to any system of belief involving reincarnation.

burglar: Like mortuary assistant, slaughterman, murderer, etc. *Burglar* is one of the Mouseboks' preferred professions. See *Money*.

Or a good way of stimulating mental alertness among other Mousebokses may be to feign employment as a Burglar. This course may encourage various disadvantages – see *Murder*. Imagined and *Supernatural* Burglars feature often in *Nightmares* and *Fears*.

dark: An elongation of terror in closing eyes before *Sleep* and/or *Death*.

death: The termination of an inexhaustible source of *Despair*. A constant breeding-ground of both creeping and seizing *Fears*. Good subject for meditation – see *Night*, see also *Murder*.

despair: A kind of relaxation. Also taken to be a sure sign of intellectual development among Mousebokses.

devil: An excellent subject for *Night* meditations. See *What You Deserve*.

Or something a Mouseboks had better know. Hence the phrase 'Better the Devil you know' which brings faint but constant comfort to the few surviving Mousebokses afflicted by religious inclinations.

dreams: The perfect medium in which to imagine bearing *Arms* against Mouseboks Family members.

family: Spending time within the Mouseboks Family might be likened to drifting in an open boat filled with cannibals precisely at tea-time. Their company is always enlivening and their interest in others very sincere, if not deeply alarming.

fears: Life's constant companions, shapers of our destiny and characters. Their manifestations are infinitely various including: creeping, leaping, looming, seizing, stunting, sweating, paralysing, stupefying, hypnotising and doom-laden. A *Fear* may be laxative, expectorant, emetic or simply felling. Numbing fears are rarely experienced but frequently wished for.

Note that a combination of elongated *Fears* may constitute a kind of vocation for many older Mousebokses.

Although *Fears* may be affected by the presence or absence of daylight, money, certain individuals, etc. they very largely have full and independent lives of their own. The hobbies and gathering places of temporarily absent or inactive *Fears* would be a major topic of philosophical discussion between Mousebokses, were they not afraid to mention them.

fears of the dark: These particular *Fears* are of such a rich and varied character among Mousebokses that only their extreme unsociability and *Fear of Psychiatrists* has prevented them from becoming a celebrated source of Behavioural research.

fear of psychiatrists: Mousebokses pre-empt any fears of *Insanity* by constantly assuming themselves to be insane. As no mad person truly believes they are mad and Mousebokses all believe they are mad, truly, then all Mousebokses must be sane. Even the mad ones. This removes all *Fear of Psychiatrists*.

female: A recognisable condition among some Mousebokses. Will not encompass any nurturing, delicate or maternal instincts. Mouseboks Family Womenfolk generally prefer to avoid pregnancy and adopt older children, if not adults, who are preferably resident in distant countries. Homicidal levels of menstrual tension are maintained by *Female* Mousebokses for five or six weeks of the month. Noted for their quirky sense of humour.

Francis: Traditionally the first name of all Mousebokses, male and female. This has many benefits – all family insults are pleasantly inclusive and neither memory nor imagination need ever be taxed on the part of parents with regard to child naming or summoning. Convoluted arguments can be started in any assembly of Mousebokses in a matter of seconds, as all comments directed to any Mouseboks by name will quite naturally always be entirely false and entirely true – a good starting-point for many hours of invigorating bare-knuckle repartee.

future: A usefully inexhaustible source of *Despair* and *Fear*, terminated only by *Death*.

God: Mousebokses have a deep and working belief in God which has, for many generations, meant that Mousebokses do not generally pray at all for *Fear* that God will hear where they are and come to get them.

guilt: An unfamiliar concept.

It has long troubled churchmen and moralists to find that Mousebokses, though constantly racked by nauseous waves of *Guilt*, continue to commit unspeakable acts of every guilt-inducing shade and variety. This seems a dreadful and shaking denial of *Natural Justice*.

This disturbance to the spiritual equilibrium of so many devout men is a huge source of satisfaction to all Mousebokses, although tremendous guilt prevents them from celebrating it too openly.

hands: Those things which we hold for each other, while wishing our arms were longer.

insanity: An affliction exclusively confined to others, particularly those in authority. For exceptions, see *Fear of Psychiatrists*.

last straw: Given the prevalence of *Despair* and *Fear* in the Mouseboks Family, any straw will always be the last. Or Mouseboks family members never use straws, this being regarded as a waste of good drinking time and suction.

life: Like an overbearingly scented rubber ice pick, a chocolate pacemaker, or an open tub of chicken giblets cast out to a man besieged by tetchy sharks. That is to say, a gift of very little utility, which draws on lengthy and unpleasant ramifications.
See *Bad Joke*.
See also *What You Deserve*.
See also *Nightmares* (Waking).

lust: A word unfamiliar to Mousebokses, of indefinable meaning, with accusatory overtones. As Mousebokses regard all other Mouseboks Family members, all members of any other family and all animals exceeding 18″ in any direction as insensible subjects for perverse and graphic experiment they have not found it necessary to develop what would essentially be a synonym for *Normality*.

marriage: A kind of bedroom ceasefire without benefit of UN Peacekeeping Forces. See *Fear of Psychiatrists, Money, Murder, Odd Noises, Sex*.

masturbation: Another word for *Self-Respect*. Or substitute for central heating in older Mouseboks homes. See *Sex*, See *Fear of Psychiatrists*.

money: Something to light the heart. A family symbol of reliability, warmth, affection self-esteem and dignity. Should be easy to fold. See *Mouseboks*.

Mouseboks: A curious name, taken by the Mouseboks Family in a never-repeated moment of unanimity brought on by group shock.

Before they developed their new name, the Mousebokses were once gathered together (see *Bad Joke, Death, Murder*) in the house of an *Old Aunt*. The *Old Aunt* was expected to die within the month and slowly all the possibly relevant inheriting Mousebokses had gathered in the *Old Aunt's* house for *Fear* of other Mousebokses beating them to the will, or rather its contents.

It was common knowledge that the Mouseboks' Aunt kept a huge amount of *Money* in her attic, carefully locked and multiply-bolted against *Burglars* and other Mousebokses. On her death, this *Money* would become free and legally open to her *Family*.

Perhaps speeded on her way by the presence of so many Family members, the *Old Aunt* duly died and, as her last breath soaked into the wallpaper, an eager horde of Mousebokses stormed her attic, only hindered by another mob of Mousebokses engaged in removing her furniture.

This was, and still remains, standard funerary procedure. In a day or two the Aunt would be remembered and packed off in a plywood box to an inexpensive resting-place in a Mouseboks allotment but, meanwhile, the real, financial business of dying was under way.

After only a few hours, the eager Mouseboks horde bit, scratched, drilled, kicked and sledge-hammered their way into the attic. There, glimmering in the dusty dormer windowed light, were scores of open cases filled with more scores of little cardboard boxes all stacked neatly and bound with elastic bands. Inside these the Mousebokses would find their *Money*.

At this juncture several Mouseboks menfolk were heard to pray — something only ever done by Mousebokses who are in the presence of their own certain death or unthinkable amounts of money. The Mouseboks womenfolk did likewise and were heard to weep openly — an entirely novel occurrence.

In one, huge, spontaneous lunge the cases were disembowelled, the boxes snapped for and torn open and inside was found:

Almost nothing at all.
Fat Mice.
Dead, happy mice.

Mouse droppings.

Mouse processed note dust.

And one final gathering of twenty-three notes, rusted holes where the old Aunt's staples had fixed them together, long before.

The family was not the same after that. Or, to be precise, it was much more like itself than it had ever been before. And it took the name Mouseboks as a constant reminder that nothing in life worth waiting for should ever be delayed for even a moment. Young Mousebokses are also reminded of this one dreadful occasion when courtesy and ingenious locks prevented the Mouseboks *Family* from getting what it wanted.

This has never happened again.

murder: Something else to light the heart. Whenever a Mouseboks is discovered, solitary and smiling, s/he will most assuredly be engaged in meditations upon murder. A Mouseboks, solitary and laughing, will be engaged in meditations upon murdering another Mouseboks. A Mouseboks, solitary and dancing while dribbling help-lessly with mirth, will be engaged in meditations upon murdering another Mouseboks for money.

mysterious additions: Not in themselves supernatu-ral. Simply the ability of any Mouseboks family member to perform any kind of simple or complex arithmetic to his or her financial benefit, notwithstanding circumstances of logic and fairness.

natural justice: A phrase almost perfectly describing the contents of an unforseeably emptied diving pool. That is to say, something which is not only almost nothing, but also painful. See *Bad Joke, Life, What You Deserve*.

night: Hours spent in staying uncomfortably awake. Also natural home of *Nightmares, Sneaking Mousebokses, Burglars, Odd Noises* and *Fears of the Dark*.

nightmares: The natural consequence of sleep. May involve loss of *Money* or being murdered by other Mouseboks *Family* members. May also be Waking, see *Life*.

normality: See *What You Deserve*.
   Also a disturbing quality, always to be distrusted in others — particularly those bearing religious pamphlets. Like bad breath, dimples and leprosy, may cause onset of low *Self-Respect*. See *Money*. See also, *Sex*.

odd noises: Might include the full repertoire of vomiting (including the counter-tenor), spattering whines, ugly crunches, unexpected breathing and sentimental serenades. A kind of informally arranged entertainment to help speed on the *Family*'s uniformly sleepless nights. Infinitely less threatening than *Odd Silences*. See *Burglar*, *Fear*, *Money*, *Murder*.

odd silences: Almost infallible precursor of attack by *Sneaking Mousebokses*, *Burglars*, or other persons engaged in *Murder* and similar enterprises, Major cause of *Fear*.

rules: The Mouseboks Family, like many others, has developed a large number of more or less useful and applicable Rules for Living. Among these are:

If in doubt, blame Francis.

Because you are mad, I am not. (Many variants on this theme.)

Because I think I am mad, I am not.

Whatever you do, don't get caught.

If you do get caught, don't tell us.

Love is Godless, God is loveless and everything is as bad as you always suspected.

Three things never to share: confidences, feelings and second hand swabs.

Trust is the luxury of idiots and children.

Betray your children often, and they may learn and grow.

Fear is the luxury of adults.

Feed your fears in darkened places, that they may learn and grow and be with you always, for ever and ever amen.

A life without fear is a life without reality.

Hating other people will always be healthy and useful, as long as you hate yourself more. It's fairer that way.

Ask the family, when you die, to bury you face down in a cast iron coffin and cut off your feet. You'll still come back and haunt them — everyone does.

Be happy. See *Where it Gets You*.

sex: A good replacement for conversation. (In many Mouseboks marriages conversation has, in fact, never been found necessary.)

Or good way of meeting strangers.

Or replacement for any other area of a Mouseboks Family member's life which may currently be lacking or faintly disappointing.

Or small word for anything deeply unpleasant with huge and unimaginably ghastly consequences.

Note that withdrawal of Sex for more than eight hours is not recommended for Mousebokses. See *Fear of Psychiatrists*.

self-respect: Exists as the exact inverse of respect held for others. May also be in direct proportion to wealth of Mouseboks in question. See *Money*. Also see *Masturbation*. Also see *Sex*.

sleep: Last resort of the sadly demented. Or a condition of having exhausted all of life's possibilities. See *Dark, Despair, Lust, Masturbation, Money, Murder, Sex.*

sneaking Mousebokses: A Mouseboks at his/her most comfortable, given the contents of his/her brain, will always appear to be Sneaking. A *Sneaking Mouseboks* will always be completely silent unless s/he is playing a complicated double bluff which may involve crashing round an occupied Mouseboks household late at night, dressed as a *Burglar*. See *Murder*. Such systems of bluff, double bluff and counter bluff can lead a number of Mousebokses into a state of fatal cerebral collapse. See *Anticipation.*

supernatural: Belief in the Supernatural is not permitted in any Mouseboks Family member. Supernatural phenomena are regarded as the *Last Straw, Normality* being bad enough, never mind any further *Mysterious Additions.*

thinking: A very flexible word, can have many meanings, including, plotting, nursing *Murder* in one's heart, dying, suffering from a felling *Fear*, a fatal cerebral collapse, a paralysing *Lust*, or simply indigestion.

May also be used in the phrase, 'Go away, I'm thinking.' See *Masturbation, Murder, Odd Noises, Sex.* Time and experience have meant that young Mousebokses are now not encouraged to think at all. Mouseboks Family thinking at its most highly developed may be likened to a piping hot iron fist, tucked up in a cosy mitten of electrified brass.

uncles/cousins/brothers: A kind of cosmic balancing point for imagination and reality – their earthly manifestation is always the exact reverse of the image cultivated by others in their absence.

Mouseboks Family *Brothers* never dress in cardigans and waistcoats, do not smoke pipes, or love small children and pets, nor do their *Uncles* have pockets inexhaustibly filled with fresh boiled sweets, chocolate and peppermints, nor do their *Cousins* have any discernible loving, altruistic or even minimally human qualities.

Mouseboks Family menfolk smoke poisonous and illegal roll-ups, dress as they would have been afraid to when they were twenty years younger, cannot be trusted with any young person, or any older person, or any pet of any sex, will borrow and steal money, drink, medicines, pets, spouses and any likely-looking ornaments and will urinate indiscriminately both indoors and out, blaming any resultant distress on whatever small children/pets or passing strangers are available. See *Anticipation, Lust, Murder, Sex, Money, What You Deserve.*

what for: A question perfectly describing what the questioner will receive on having asked it. An example of the neatness and natural economy of Mouseboks Family Thinking. Phrase only used by very young Mousebokses.

what you deserve: A random but always negative
quantity.

where it gets you: Nowhere at all.

FRIDAY PAYDAY

WAITING HERE, WITH nothing to sit on was a bugger. You could sit, if you wanted, on the brick edge of the flower bed, but that would make you dirty; earth and chewing-gum and that. Folk stubbed out their chewing-gum on the bricks, it was disgusting.

Because of the rain, it was muddy this evening and she would have to watch herself more than usual, because she had on the fawn skirt and the cream-coloured jacket. They were nice, but they showed the slightest thing and she liked to keep clean.

Later, she would be tired, but just now, she felt very settled and quiet inside. She was here.

A block of faces came out to the sunlight, coats and hair rising in the breeze and she watched them. She knew how to watch.

Sometimes, there was a girl who was a dancer. This station must be near to where she lived. It was only a guess, but she ought to be a dancer. You could see in the way she walked, as though clothes were unnecessary. She was too thin, but she had a lovely face and, if she was stripped bare naked she probably wouldn't look even a wee bit undressed. Her skin would be enough, better than clothes.

It would always be a good night if you saw her. The dancer was lucky.

The faces passed more quickly than you would think. That was always the way. From the top of the steps until they reached her, she could count to seven slowly. Up to nine and they were beyond her, crossing the road and turning, going away.

No one had stopped this time. No one had really seen her, or hesitated. But they would. It was early yet, and the dancer hadn't come.

It was funny how people could tell why she was waiting. In the way she could tell the dancer was a dancer. It was the same. Some people would see her waiting here and they would be able to tell.

At first, she had only noticed them, noticing her, and hadn't known why, or who they were. Now she could recognise all the types before they had moved from the shadow of the entrance and walked past the poster for young persons' travel cards. Some of them did nothing. They looked at her or looked away, smiling, frowning, pretending she wasn't there. Some of them did what she needed. Needing wasn't hoping or wanting, but if they did what she was needing, then that was enough.

By the time it was fully dark, the first one had come and gone. They had walked together to the car park and stayed in his car, without driving away. Then she walked back alone to the station and stood. She waited.

Twenty pounds, ten minutes. He had been English, which she preferred. The Arab-looking ones had more money, but they frightened her. Scots were always somehow rougher, although she was Scottish too.

She was Scottish and here was London, Whittington's place, fucking Dick's place, but it didn't make much of a difference – most people she met didn't seem to come from here. They were all strangers together.

It did feel different, though. Out in this bit, the houses were all small with their own tiny gardens, too tiny to be any use. White walls and square, little windows looking over grass like green paper and stupid dots of flowers – all of it only there to make a point. The people walked past her in the street and didn't like her, but she wasn't sure of why that was. They might be able to tell that she was Scottish; they might not like her waiting. They should have been nicer to her, really; she was only wee. And a stranger. Folk were dead unfriendly here.

Of course, this was a Friday night and the amateurs were out – just school kids making money for the weekend. She didn't like to wait near them – get messed up. Soon she'd go into the station and ride to town. The town was more like Glasgow – a proper city. Big, glass buildings and hamburger places and lights. Very bright, but very strange where the lights were and very black over everything else. She just dreeped down in between

NOW THAT YOU'RE BACK

the two. The black to hide and the bright to show. The city was very ideal for her lifestyle.

Going down the escalator, she passed the dancer who looked tired.

The underground could be scarey. Not because of people – because of itself. She didn't like the push of wind when the train came up to the platform. She didn't like the noises. Even in the Glasgow underground, which was wee, she had been scared and this one would go where that fire had been – all those people underground and burning – like the coal in the shut-down mines. She closed her eyes as the carriages slid beside her. They opened their doors.

MIND   THE   GAP.

Sometimes, that was a tape-recording, but sometimes it was a real person, trying to talk like a tape-recording, she'd noticed that.

Inside, when it started moving, she sat away from either end, in case there was a crash, or else she stood near a door and held on with her feet apart which made you more steady, even with heels.

She wasn't frightened often. Sometimes they would ask her if she was scared. Scared of them. If they wanted her to say so, she would tell them she was, but she wasn't. For a person of her age, she was very brave. For a person of her age she was fucking older than anyone she knew.

The Hotel Man had believed she was scared of him,

but that was just because she let him; it wasn't true. Not really true. Also, she'd known he would have had to make her frightened if he hadn't thought she was frightened and she'd known he would like to do that. Just for peace and quietness, it was best if she made him think she was already scared.

She'd known he was going to be that way from the beginning — breathing and looking at her and trying to make her afraid. He came to her room in the morning on the fifth day she was there and said she would have to pay her bill or clear off out of it. He shouted and spoke about policemen and what they would do. Send her home, or lock her up and bodysearch her.

Locking up would be better than home. The same, but better.

Whenever he spoke to her, the Hotel Man breathed funny, through his mouth. He looked at her and breathed the way her mother had told her she ought to if she had onions to chop. If you breathed through your mouth, they wouldn't make you cry.

The Hotel Man breathed like you should for chopping onions when he told her about the polis and asked about her money and what could she suggest she ought to do. In her silence, he watched and breathed. Nobody was crying then and when she did, the following day, she was crying because of her mother, not because of him or being scared. She couldn't help crying, she was sad. She knew she would never be as good as her mother was now. Her skin would never be as nice, or her fingers – her Ma'd had clever hands. She couldn't even cook, it didn't work. It didn't taste good. It wouldn't matter if she practised, there would always be something missing from what she did and now she wouldn't be able to practise any more. Cooking had seemed dead important then, she didn't know why.

The Hotel Man was stupid, he hadn't understood. He was just satisfied with believing he'd made her cry. But he couldn't ever do that, wouldn't know where to begin.

Coming up out of the station, the wind was rising, growing unpredictable. Different parts of a newspaper were diving and swinging in the air and there were whirls of smaller rubbish scraping the foot of the walls. It felt like something starting, maybe a hurricane again.

The last hurricane in London had come when she was still in Glasgow. In school, they'd had to write about it and she'd been sad because of all the ruined trees. Her father had said there'd been a hurricane once in Glasgow, but nobody'd cared.

That was all in the autumn, after the third time she'd run to other places and before the fourth. The fourth time, she'd made it to London and the Hotel Man.

He'd been like her father. Only he'd called it testing the goods when he did it and he'd made her take him out of herself and rub him. He'd put it in her throat so she'd thought she would die, couldn't breathe, didn't know how to manage yet. Her father had been more sleekit. He'd climbed through the window from the street one afternoon and showed himself to her by accident on purpose. That was badness, she just had to accept that there was badness in people, like that.

Their sitting-room windows were opened right up and into the street and she could see other folk she knew, by their windows, sitting on the pavement or standing in their rooms. Her father was wearing shorts and trainers, nothing else, and he sat astride the window frame and smiled at her, let his shorts ride up.

It didn't seem right that all those people were there, just beyond the window.

Father called it having a cuddle and said it was her mother's fault. He'd used to do this with her mother but then she'd gone to somewhere else and he still needed someone because he was a normal man.

From then she'd always wanted to be somewhere else. It made you need a different place to be, getting stuck with a normal man. Then you got a different place and you were still wrong, because you were wanting a different time and to be a different person.

This was payday Friday, end of the month, which was usually the busiest time. After the fifth or sixth, she had a wee sit and something to eat. The gale was getting worse. It wasn't cold especially, but some of the gusts were so strong that when you faced them, you couldn't breathe.

Watching through the big glass panel with her coffee, she saw everything turning unsteady, losing control. It didn't feel dangerous now she was out of it, just weird. Like being drunk without drinking.

She had a choice of places to go to for a bit of peace: chicken places, or pizza places, hamburger places, all kinds of places. She preferred to go where they sold doughnuts because doughnuts had no smell. If you kept them in the napkin, your hands stayed clean and when you'd finished, your mouth was sweet. Folk didn't mind a wee bit sweetness on your lips. If you smelled of grease and vinegar, curry sauce or something, you'd get nowhere. Not with the ones who noticed these things and those were the ones you should want.

She had seen women talking to men they met in the doughnut place, but you couldn't do that, they might not let you in again. She wouldn't do work here, anyway, this was her place, where she could rest. That was a decision she'd made. She could have let ones take her in here and let them look like they could have been her father or her uncle – these would be ones who had thought she looked hungry, or cold, or wanted feeding up. They would take her here and feed her, be her daddy for a while, and then they would take her away and be strangers again. They were probably really poofs or something. She preferred to be here on her own.

A little crowd gusted in, on the way home from something, almost falling, hair wild, laughing. She smelled their mixture of perfumes, examined their clothes. One of the women looked at her and smiled, as the party sat down, then the man next to her whispered something short and she turned away.

Along the wall and away from the window, there were boys in tracksuits, drinking coffee. You could tell they all knew each other, although they were sitting split up between different tables. Once they were outside, they would get louder and walk together, filling the street. She didn't look at them and didn't avoid them, she just accepted they were there. You couldn't tell what people like that might do. You couldn't tell what a group of them might wait outside to do. They weren't bad; only nosey. You didn't want to be something they had to find out about.

Danny wouldn't be pleased about this; her sitting around on her arse all night and not making him money. That was his fault for needing a lot. He said it was for medicine, but any cunt knew what kind of medicine that was.

She had nothing to do with that. Up at home, you were always getting offered that, anything, their mammy's tablets, anything, and she hadn't touched it then and she wouldn't now except for when her nerves were nipping. It was fucking stupid. He was just boring now. She could dress any way she wanted, he didn't care any more − he didn't even talk to her, or eat the food she got. She tried to look after him properly, but he didn't want it, he only wanted the money and the shite he was using now. He'd made love to her before — not the other stuff — and he'd been different and really lovely. He'd used to hold her and kiss and say the nice places in Scotland where they'd live when everything was fixed. Ha ha.

They were going to go back home with their money. It would be great to go back with money, old enough for folk to hear you and with money. She would have a baby and she would take excellent care of it and call it James or maybe Mary, like her mother. Ha ha ha.

Now Danny was shooting up, she wouldn't have his fucking baby. Couldn't be putting up with that shite altogether. She'd been so fucking careful, making people take precautions, trying really fucking hard to make all of them take precautions, and he didn't even know what she was talking about and now he was sticking needles anywhere he'd seen a vein. Sometimes she hoped he would just die, better if they all did — if they all lay out with the folk who were skippering and then in the morning the polis would come and brush them all away.

The last of her coffee tasted bogging. She might as well leave it. It was alright to do that here, there were unfinished doughnuts and napkins, paper cups across most of the tables. The floor wasn't clean, either. Every now and then, a girl would come and clear things away. She looked crabbit and sick, very yellow — doing the kind of job you took when you couldn't get anything else.

Most of the staff here were black. She couldn't get over that. Every time you went to places here, the people who served you and cleaned up after you were black. It must be like this in South Africa.

The times when she thought of stopping it, of really doing something else, she always imagined having to work in here. If she was lucky, she would work in here. In two years' time, she would be old enough to get a fucking dirty job in here and work all week to earn what she could in a day, just now. So what's the point of that? All right, she didn't get the money herself. You didn't ever get the money, but you earned it, you were close to it, you knew it was yours.

And all these folk that wanted her to change and to take her away from it — they talked about qualifications and training and then they just stopped. They couldn't make sense of it either. They asked you what you wanted to do and then stopped — just lies or nothing — because nothing they could give you would be better than what you'd got.

She knew what she was qualified for — hand relief or up the kilt. That's what the Hotel Man called it — up the kilt — because she was Scottish and he wasn't. Fancied himself as a comic. Fancied himself like they all did, saying they were being careful but cheating all the same, still treating you like a wean.

Something hard clattered against the window and birled

away. It seemed to wake her from something. Like she'd been staring at the street without seeing for ages. Everything outside that could be was in flight, floating by, and it reminded her of looking at the dentist's fish tank and of feeling scared over what was coming next.

It was past the time when she should be out there, earn Danny some more, but she felt a bit sick again, a bit hot. If she bought another coffee and sat it would pass away. She hadn't felt right since she'd left the Hotel Man. Not since she'd had his present for going away.

A man in a nice jacket turned back from the counter and smiled. It was that daft, private smile that went between two, always ugly really, even if it was for you. The woman already at the table returned it with a friendly, wee shake of her head. She was much younger than him. Probably he wouldn't mind if she was younger still. A lot of them liked their girls little which was lucky for her. Or lucky for Danny, it depended how you looked at it.

A man like that had told her she should stop it and get out. Not a man, a customer. He'd looked like a social worker when you saw him up close – the same kind of pathetic face. Trying to understand you, as if he was the only one that could.

She'd got in his car as usual and then known he was weird. He was too relaxed. There wasn't much you could do with the weird ones, except to wait and see. He'd seemed harmless.

He'd told her he would pay her, but he didn't want

anything. She told him that nobody didn't want anything. He just patted her knee and smiled.

'I made that myself. It has two secret drawers in it and a secret panel.'

He'd grinned like he was completely stupid and passed her a heavy, wooden box, with a sloping lid. The wood was pale with little pieces of darker wood, set in. She'd liked the smell of it, and the smoothness.

You shouldn't ever let them take you home. Not take you anywhere unknown, because that wasn't safe. But she let him drive her to his home and take her in. He made her steak and beans and baked potato, because that's what she felt like asking for. He gave her wine when she'd asked for voddy, but she drank it. Then he gave her the box.

'See if you can find the drawers.'

'I'm not a kid.'

'OK. Don't. I've got a video I want to watch. If you don't mind.'

'Canny sleep?'

'Not now, no. I want to see this film. Then you can tell me all about yourself.'

He smiled, as if that was a funny thing to say.

When she woke up, he was looking at her. He told her she must have been tired and she nodded. The TV wasn't on, which meant he must have been watching her, instead of the video. So he was pervy, like she'd thought.

'You're not too well, are you? Do you know why?'

She shook her head, thinking that of course she knew why. She didn't eat like he did, or have a clean bed like he did, or live in a nice flat. She wasn't well because of rats and damp and dirtiness in Danny's squat, because there wasn't a toilet there, not even water to wash or anything. London wasn't like 'My Fair Lady' but you could tell, just by listening to him, that he thought it was and he was going to try and be Rex Harrison or some shite like that. Looked nothing like him.

The man kept on looking at her. You could see he was concentrating on being kind and getting her to talk, people liked to hear about things sometimes, but she wasn't going to tell him anything. It was none of his business, not even if he had paid for her time. Was this him trying to check if she was clean? Stupid if he was.

'Don't you think you deserve a bit better than this? Someone your age? You shouldn't be stuck with this. You need a future.'

No she did not. A future? All that time, all the same? She didn't need that.

'I'm nineteen, I can do what I like.'

'I didn't ask how old you were. I could tell you how old I think you are. Maybe fifteen. I could tell you how much older you already look, but you know that.'

She watched him think of something else to say.

'You're not from round here. Where are you from?'

Maybe if she lifted her skirt that would shut him up. Then he wouldn't feel sorry for her. Then he'd stop trying so hard to respect her.

Not even the Hotel Man had done that – he'd only shown her the way things had to be done. When he'd found out she was leaving him, he'd locked her in her room. She'd been there for almost a day when he took her down to the where the boilers were. It was night and the hotel above her was quiet. The men sitting round the walls were quiet too, drinking and waiting for her. The Hotel Man did it first, and then he left.

It was maybe the following afternoon when she knew he'd come back again. Except she was in a different place then, in her room on top of the bed. She was dirty into her bones, stiff with it. Bastards. Only some folk were bastards, but she'd met the whole fucking pack of them at once.

He told her she had half an hour to leave. She was going because he'd decided she would – that was the way it worked – she did what other people decided, just accept it.

She looked along the couch at the man. He was still staring at her.

'I've got nothing to tell you. You want me to go?'

'No, that's alright. Now you're here, you might as well stay.'

Which meant he'd decided what to do.

When they'd finished he brought sheets and stuff to the sofa. He tucked her in. Well, she hadn't expected he'd let her sleep in his bed, she wasn't clean. But he kissed her a lot, on the mouth and on the stomach – like she'd thought, pervy.

In the morning, he gave her cereal and toast for breakfast and coffee which she didn't drink. She didn't let him drive her back, because she felt sad again and that should be private. When she left, he squeezed her hand and watched until she'd turned the corner of the street. She wished he'd gone inside straight away.

It had took her ages to walk back to town. Danny hadn't been there when she got in and it was better without him. She knew that she wanted to stay where she was and have Danny go somewhere else. That would make her lonely, but it would be best.

With the money that she'd kept from Danny and what she'd earned tonight, she could go back home. She could go up for a while and stay and then come back when she felt different. She wouldn't do this in Glasgow, only here, so she could only stay for a short while and then come back, because you had to work, look after yourself. Sometimes she just got dead homesick – adverts on the underground for Scotland, they lied like fuck, but they still made you think.

THE BOY'S FAT DOG

I'VE BEEN LISTENING here all day and I can hear for miles. I told that to someone this morning and got no answer. Perhaps I muttered. People have told me I mutter from time to time and it has never been important because I have never had anything very much to say. It doesn't matter today if no one heard me because I was mainly only speaking to myself. I know what I know and what I know is the idea that came in my head that there is a clearness up here for listening far away to dogs and motors and children which are all down there.

I'm the one who found this place so it belongs to me. I wouldn't say that one out loud, but I know that it's true. The decision was mine to bring us here. I could have seen the houses and let them be or I could have been less careful in looking and maybe not come this far because the boot on my left foot is uncomfortable and I would rather not walk as much as I do. Only I did come and I did look and I did see and there it all was.

These houses were waiting with the little roads and the people and those nice trees which will bear apples, I think. They have no blossom, but I think they will be apple trees and have fruit in the autumn. I couldn't say how soon that will be. I have not needed to know for a while what time of year it is. I no longer seem to do the things that gave shape to my year, but the days are still days, just the same, whether I bother about them or not. I have no grip of time, but it holds me. The weather is often a clue, of course, but not always reliable, I personally find it very vague. Peasant people, country people, like the ones down there would be able to read the sky and the animals and know just when and where they are. They probably sniff the air and know what time of day it is precisely.

There are country people up here too, but none of us seem to remember how to be that way. We are all so cleaned by being here that such considerations seem impossible.

I have binoculars with me although I never use them much, they spoil my feel of the space. With my eyes I can watch a little coloured dab move and understand it is a boy in a coat so red it smears up into the air above him. And I can hear every word he whispers to his black barrel dog, but I can hold up one finger in front of my eyes and both of them are gone. That's reality, that's the way this is. Up here we see them and we know them and we know what to do with them and they are ignorant and little, hardly anything at all.

I have no interest in peering and sneaking up to shutters, magnifying my way into cow-breathed widow parlours. A little glimpse of hair, a nipple, something to gulp about, some of them still want that, but not me. This isn't the time to be close, this is the time to be outside and above and to feel things as they really are because there are some truths even I can recognise and one of them must be perspective. Up here I have perspective and it makes me peaceful and free. Someone yesterday was saying he'd lost his reason. I don't understand that, it being such a contrast to my own condition here.

I have reason, without it I wouldn't have come. The news of this was everywhere — full of reasons. Written and spoken and we saw the photographs, heard the plans and these terrible rumours and it was clear that no one could be excluded from this on any side. I remember thinking 'This is total. This is the most total thing we will ever see. I must be total with it.' That felt fine.

I know I have experience of the world and of being lied to. But no one would lie about this — that would be more than a sin, that could never be forgiven, it would be too big — and if they had tried to lie then I would know. I am nothing but honesty now and I would know. Doing this is as honest as I can be. I catch myself thinking some times and really appreciating how clear this all makes me feel inside.

I had to leave my home and the girls and my job — selling shoes, although that seems unlikely now. I find it completely impossible to imagine a shoe shop today.

Nobody said anything openly, not at first, they were being gentle or shy, but we knew what they intended all the same. We were being asked to go out and kill these people before they could kill any more of us. There can be none of them left, because they have crossed a kind of line and become animal, machine, something unhuman and only concerned with killing people like me who have homes and rows of winter greens, two little girls, a red-haired wife and jobs that don't quite suit them.

My brother would have lain down and died for a chance like this. He was much more involved in things than me, you would have said he was political or that he had that kind of pride in something you could put a flag to. But I'm not here on his behalf, that would be stupid. This is for my girls. We never were a religious family, but they should have the chance to have their own God. No one else's. I have no pretensions of grace for myself, God won't be any friend of mine.

I am no friend of mine. I am sure of that. I can see my arm, see the cuff of the shirt I used to wear at home. It seems impossible that it can be with me here — just the same thing as it was, more dirty, frayed a little, but the same. My wife might recognise me in this shirt, but I would not, because I know that I am different. My shirt has outlived me, I am the one that wore away.

And I can look down there at the house with pigs behind it and the brown door and I can watch myself, without closing my eyes, slitting the throats of pigs and pigs and pigs. The noise and the warm and the sputter, the give. That was how I practised.

If I dream now, I see the pigs more often than the people — the pigs were good animals and most of the meat went to waste which I am sorry for. Or I see a little boy. He wriggled and I cut his face which was not what I intended. I see him at night.

Also at night I think that God must want this because nothing can happen without God. If there is God, It must want this kind of mess, even for people who have a real faith. Like when things will flip open sometimes in my head at those two brothers praying while we did what we did — the stuff with the women. There God allowed us to contradict the power of prayer with these old, old habits we all at once remember. We have terrible, necessary ways of saying — saying these people are nothing and even those ways mean nothing to us. One way or another, it always means nothing, what we do, and God lets it be like that. Meaningless.

Which is what I'm used to. I've always been accustomed to live for others and not on my own behalf. I've taken care of my family, now in this way more than ever. Doing this means they will be able to go on living and be as they are. I know I loved them when I saw them last and that I do this out of love for them, but I think I will not love them any more. I get angry with them and with God and my boot. Equal anger for each and it's all useful in the end because when I go down to the houses, the people there will get it. I'll burn it away in them, put the plastic bags over their faces and set the fire and watch them melt.

That's what I do. It's good for me to let go that way. I don't know why, but it's good.

The boy's fat dog down there, I would claim that. It wouldn't like me, naturally, and I couldn't travel with it, but I've taken a fancy to the thing. Too old to bark, too heavy to run away, I get a sick feeling watching it and knowing the way it'll end.

We will come down the slope tonight, where the stream is, fast and quiet and I will try to be careful, even though we know there are no men here, not to speak of. I've seen our people killed by women and grandfathers, children with unmanageable guns – you would think they might die a little more willingly, not having the proper strength or skills to resist us correctly, but that's not the case. They despair very quickly and that makes them wicked. Dying to save each other, they'll thrash about and kill you with something so unexpected and ridiculous it'll make you tired to think of it.

I will drop down, bounce and bounce, the sound of me and what I have with me, always the same. The closer I get, the longer the distance – it will gape for the last few yards, shrink me right down and make me angry. Without the hill to stand on, I get small. just like them. I leave the clean, running air and break through the band of house smoke, house stink, right into the smell of them, their taste, and then I know that I am not like them, I am sure of that, because I am living and they will die. The air comes clear after that, smooth, almost on them, the real presence. I never see that too well, except in blinks and flashes. That doesn't matter, what I miss, I'll dream over again.

I think that perhaps in the dark the dog won't get it. Black dog, it could have a chance.

WARMING MY HANDS
AND TELLING LIES

'BUT IT'S SUCH a wonderful idea.'

'Do you think so?'

'Yes. I mean, ten years ago — to have written that. The millionaire's house invaded by all the animals his jungle road had killed. Wonderful.'

'They weren't real animals.'

'Well, of course not, but you made that clear. The thing is, you made them have the effect that real animals would, I mean, we felt for them.'

'Felt sorry for them.'

'Of course. We were sorry. Those eyes always watching him; the constant sound of their feet. When that tiny armadillo drowns . . .'

'It drowns in the millionaire's toilet.'

'I know.'

'And you actually think that works.'

'Yes, I've said, haven't I? I think it's a wonderful story.'

'Mm hm. They're still making roads through the jungle, they're still killing animals, destroying indigenous tribes.'

'Well, one story . . .'

'Exactly. One story wouldn't change that. You're right.'

She was peering at him again, he didn't like that. She peered the way she might at a cloudy fish bowl, checking to see if something was still alive. He wondered what she was checking for in him.

'I know you didn't mean to say it, but you're right. There isn't any point in writing, because it does no good. It does nothing at all.'

'But that . . .'

'Means that I've wasted my life. That's right. Is that what you came to find out?'

'No.'

'Then why did you come?'

Well now, he was sure he'd told her why. He couldn't have been so nervous he hadn't said. He told her before he arrived, before he even came to Dublin. He wouldn't have come all this way without telling her first: a brief, careful letter, her glorious reply and then the phone call. Hearing that voice, almost unable to answer when she spoke that name, her name. She knew why he was here. She was being confusing, making him argue, making him say things he hadn't meant. It wasn't how he remembered her at all.

But, to be honest, how did he remember her? Monagh Cairns. Novelist and critic, Monagh Cairns.

She had come to his school one Friday and read some stories. He could only recall a part of one.

Each night, the men and women of the city would go to sleep. Before they climbed into their beds, parents would kiss their children and weep and then they would walk, round shouldered, to lie under thin, cold blankets and wait. Sometimes wives and husbands would hold hands.

Each night, in one or two of the low, dark houses something very terrible would occur. Folk would point at darkened windows in the morning, they would stare at bolted doors. They would say, 'The Industrialists came there.'

He had written it down, maybe twenty times, each time slightly different, but mostly the same and although he had searched through every source he knew, he had never found a story by Monagh Cairns with a passage like it. He had never found a story about night-time disfigurements, or invisible creatures called Industrialists. Perhaps he imagined it.

He hadn't imagined her. Lovely. He never could have imagined anyone so lovely.

Thanks to his later researches, he knew that she must have been forty or thirty-nine when he saw her first. Her second and final husband had left her that spring and she still had no children. She never would. Next spring, her third collection would be published. Good reviews. For another six years, she would stay in Scotland, then she would go to Ireland and fade out of sight.

He had been seventeen and when she arrived on that Friday, he was already waiting and watching and listening hard. He was there to make up for the others. Front row desk. He would show them he was good at this. They wouldn't understand her the way he did. He read things, literature.

She surely must have noticed him when she stood so close to his desk. And maybe she had felt something too. He'd wanted her to feel how ready he was to know exactly what she meant, prepared to be outstanding for her, because she was outstanding, too. Mr Harrison had already told them she was a writer – she did that and nothing else. He couldn't imagine what that must be like.

By the end of the afternoon, she had read them three stories, one of them very short and all about love. They were still in the silence after that story, having heard a woman talking, with their accent, about fears and excitements that didn't seem even likely in someone so old. She really knew about love. One of the girls made noises as if she might cry, showing off.

Miss Cairns; Monagh – you were allowed to call her Monagh – had asked them all a question.

'Are any of you interested in writing?'

He didn't put up his hand. Nobody did, but he wanted to, he wanted to very much. He had always prayed for a moment that would alter the whole of his life and now it had come. That question. Her question had made it come. Something hot seemed to fill him and he knew this was it, for sure. He imagined the change must be howling out of his ears and down his nose. His hair must be starting to lift and he didn't dare open his mouth, for fear of something luminous bursting out.

Monagh kept on speaking and he tried to catch her eye so that she would see him and know, by the way he was sitting, that really he wanted to write. As he remembered it now, she did look his way.

'Why did you come, David? I can call you David?'

She didn't seem very different, even today. Her hair was still a blonde that could be grey, or vice versa. It was long but wound about itself and sat very neat on her head. Once he had seen her wear a French plait in a television interview and there were photographs of her with a page boy cut and a perm. Sitting now in her living-room it was odd to have only one possible image of her. She seemed, somehow, less convincing like this.

Of course, time had passed and that did make for changes. After the move to Dublin, there had been no more photographs and five years had left her face surprisingly old. Monagh's mouth seemed smaller and the line of her chin had blurred. She peered.

'I came to see you, Monagh. I came . . . I thought I'd explained. The article.'

'No, I don't understand, no one would want an article about me. Not now. Scarcely then. You'd better . . . I don't know, it's all very confusing for me. I'm not used to this any more. How long are you here?'

'Two weeks.'

'Could you come back tomorrow . . . no, the day after. Come back then; on Saturday. I've been ill, you see, otherwise I wouldn't be at home. I have to work. Would you mind coming back?'

'No, that's fine, I don't want to put you out, Miss . . . Monagh. If I came after lunch?'

He'd met her first on the Tuesday, half past four, by one of the ponds in St Stephen's Green. He was to wait in front of the sign that explained the ducks. There were many varieties of duck.

The plane brought him in from Glasgow just before lunch. It didn't take an hour, not even one hour from his home to hers. He could have done it any time. If he'd had the money. Now he could afford the plane fare, just about, and one whole fortnight in a reasonable hotel.

David's room was small, mainly pink and grey. It smelled of disinfectant and chemical freshening. He filled the kettle provided and lay back on the bed, trying to let himself know he had arrived. Turbulence on the flight had left him quite unsettled, but he began to feel better now. What he should do, he should have a little tea without milk, put on the radio for music and read a few pages from 'Nobody There' – his favourite Cairns. That would put him in the mood, on her wavelength, let him get the feel of her. So to speak.

They dusted leaves from each other's backs as they walked to the car. She pulled little twigs and fragments from the sleeves of his cardigan and swiftly brushed her fingers over his hair. Before they parted to open respective doors, she paused and allowed him a chance to kiss her. He continued to walk and fumble through his keys.

He dozed for almost an hour, dreaming of parkland and hares with grey blonde fur. Monagh's forehead caught by the classroom sunlight, somewhere he saw that.

It was raining quite sharply by the time he set out for the green. He had decided to travel without an umbrella, but wearing a hat, because he felt more confident that way. Umbrellas made him uneasy, they seemed to demand the use of both his hands and he would find himself struck clumsy in the street. The hat and the long dark overcoat were much better.

He did want to look his best. For Monagh.

Striding out along the pavement, he knew he was at home with the city; dressed to fit a Joyce short story, or a fragment of Beckett prose; resonant, stylishly simple and a little out of time.

The way he had chosen took him through Merrion

Square and he wanted to stop there and look at a few of the plaques. There was one to mark the house where Yeats had lived, one for Wilde and another for Le Fanu. At school and constantly reading, he had always assumed these people were Englishmen. As with Barrie and Buchan or Sir Arthur Conan Doyle, success had made them automatically English.

He noticed the plaque for Daniel O'Connell – not a writer – but by this time he was running for the gallery steps. Over the road and through the high gate and up the path to shelter. His hat was beginning to droop and the bottoms of his trousers were clinging round his socks. He mopped his face with a handkerchief and blew his nose, his forehead stinging with cold.

He squeaked across the varnished floors, pausing in front of a high, glowering canvas which took its theme from the Book of Revelation. If David stared at it and partly closed his eyes, the overall effect was strangely warming. He remembered Monagh Cairns took 'Revelation' as a title once. Later, he passed a bust of Sheridan, looking young and tastefully dishevelled. Dead and famous and another Honorary Englishman. Beyond the final room, he found the cafe and a very large pot of tea.

'What do you mean by that?'

'English writers. Like Naomi Mitchison, Alistair MacLean – they're Scottish writers, but they're never described that way. They are assumed to be English; good equals English.'

'Well, most folk have always known that and you could argue some cases either way. It's a bit of a red herring, really, not the central issue, and what does it have to do with my work? I was never well-known enough to be Scots.'

'I wondered what you thought. I wondered if you'd ever thought of going South.'

'Instead of going West?'

He couldn't mistake it, she was laughing at him. He'd seen an odd light in her eyes before, but now she was almost giggling. In a way, it was nice to see, but now he couldn't tell if she honestly meant what she said.

'Look, David, I could have moved to England, to France, to America, the fact is, it wouldn't have worked. Nobody liked my work when I was in Scotland – don't look like that, I'm not feeling sorry for myself. I mean nobody liked it enough for me to live. I could not make a living. I always had to do other work in order to finance my writing when the other work meant that I barely had time to sleep. I wrote or worked and existed, that was all, and it wasn't worth it. I had to give up too much.

'And I couldn't move because I'm a Scottish writer. I don't mean that it's a betrayal to write elsewhere. I think it might have been, in my case, but that's not what I'm saying. The fact is that, disconnected from Scotland, I find I don't have much to write about. Scotland was my way in.

'And I get homesick.'

'But if you knew you would be homesick here and you knew you wouldn't be able to write . . . Why?'

'Because I don't care any more.'

It wasn't a good conversation to have as their first.

The rain had become a chill dust in the breeze as he found the right pond on the Green and stood in front of the sign with its painted ducks. His pause in the gallery seemed to have driven the damp against his skin. He was shivering.

Almost at once, he heard a call.

'Mr Reid, David Reid? Hello, there. Come over this side, we'll go to Bewley's, have some tea. I should have thought it would rain.'

He turned and saw her standing across the grey lake. Even at that distance, the blue of her eyes was obvious; striking, he thought. He waved, then paused for a moment before he could make for the path. Seeing her there, it had seemed quite possible he would step out on to the water and then run to meet her.

In the steamy warm of Bewley's with his second pot of tea, he watched her eat a raisin muffin, slicing it carefully into four. Sometimes she would lick her lips for crumbs and he noticed her tongue was a very pale candy floss pink. Just to ease her into talking, he outlined his Theory of the Honorary English.

'David, what do you expect from a colonised culture? The better Scottish writing gets, the less it will matter. The work will improve itself, it won't be competing with anything other than the best it can produce. It will be international.'

'You sound quite passionate.'

'Maybe.'

'But you don't want to write.'

'It isn't a question of wanting. There's no point.'

'You can't believe that.'

'Watch me.'

David didn't go back to his hotel, not straight away. He had to walk. Monagh bent towards him when they parted, but only shook his hand. No kiss. He didn't know how he felt. Monagh. Bitch. She was a disappointing bitch. Attractive in a lonely kind of way and a disappointing bitch.

It was dark and the rain was finished. As the sky cleared, the wind grew colder and he noticed he could see the stars. Looking up from the centre of Glasgow that wouldn't have been possible, but the comparison didn't please him. Dublin seemed to be the only capital that was uglier in the dark. Away from O'Connell Street the place seemed to pinch in and he wanted the nicotine and whitewash Glasgow sky. If that meant he was being parochial, he didn't really care.

What had happened to the woman? She only seemed to come alive when she was saying that her talent had no point. How could anyone enjoy just tearing their life up like that? She was almost gleeful.

If she thought her writing was pointless, then where on earth was he? Drip-feeding a literary mirage with shitey freelance journalism. He wasn't even a journalist, hadn't written a story in months. Bitch.

Tomorrow, he was invited to her house. That would have been wonderful. But now he didn't want to go. She wouldn't talk properly about writing, she was famously secretive about her private life, he had no idea why she wanted to see him again. He was mystified. And he had a piece to write about her. Did she know how hard he'd pushed to even get the chance to do it – a piece he really cared about? At the moment it would start with 'Where is she now?' and finish with 'Fucking Dublin'.

The name of the pub escaped him. Quite probably, he never knew it. He drank Guinness which he didn't like and made him sick. No one sang or spoke Gaelic, nobody laughed a hearty, Irish laugh. The faces in the gantry glass confused him. They could have been in Glasgow, his breed; sharp and dispossessed. But this was their own, independent country now, they should be changed. They had their own, Celticly twee money, their own army and

166

they should be changed. They should be able to tell him how to change.

Finally flat in his hotel bed, David couldn't get warm. Between his head aching and the deep cold in his feet, he didn't think he slept at all until the morning. He missed breakfast.

Monagh's flat, at least, was a pleasant surprise. She had the second floor in a square Victorian house built of pale brick. The street could have been in any London suburb. He climbed a flight of concrete steps and rang at a door painted crimson to match the wooden shutters and window frames. Clearly, there were still some things Monagh managed to care about.

'Bless you.'

He'd sneezed almost as soon as she opened the door.

'I thought you were looking chilled yesterday. You should be careful.'

'Thanks, it's alright. I'm mainly tired.'

That sounded more bitter than he intended. Monagh seemed to glow, while he'd spent the night in mourning for her career. Perhaps she really didn't care.

They had tea. More tea. Then:

'I should show you round. That's the kind of thing you want?'

'If you don't mind; that would be nice.'

She steered him along the hallway to the kitchen, a room he guessed would be sunny at the right time of the year. Her bedroom was almost empty. Single bed. The bathroom, too was remarkably bare, not even an old leaf dropped from the ivy plant. David was about to ask her why she didn't seem to have any books when she opened a final door. Her Bluebeard room.

It was small and made smaller by ranks of shelves. In the window was a plain oak table beside a filing cabinet.

'It's a study.'

'That's right. My study has always been like this. I take it with me.'

'From Scotland?'

'Yes, everywhere. It makes me feel at home. Don't worry, I don't use it. It's here to remind me of my mistakes; so I won't make them again. You believe you can only really learn from your past?'

'Of course. But, you honestly don't ever go in here?'

'Only to dust.'

'You . . . I'm sorry, but you seem to like suffering. Why do you keep this here?'

When she didn't answer he thought she was offended, but she only gave a closed smile and offered him more tea.

It was dark by the time he left her and he still had almost nothing to put in his story. If he didn't get somewhere with her on Saturday, he would have to give up. A whole fortnight's holiday pissed away in Dublin. His first and only foreign assignment buggered, to coin a phrase. They wouldn't even offer him expenses.

*

On Friday, David made it down to breakfast and then returned to his room, threw up and went to bed. He felt feverish. The morning and the afternoon shone through the curtains, modified by giant pink roses and their giant grey leaves and he slept. The radio played through his dreams, adding the day's news here and there while Monagh sat in her square, bare living-room and told him there was nothing he could do.

'Write yourself better, David. Alter the exchange rate, save Kuwait. You want to be a writer; you believe in all of this.'

He tried to dream her on to her bed. Her hair would lie against the crimson coverlet. Why did she like crimson so much, when it always reminded him of blood? Her skin would be on the crimson, pale as the belly of a hare. And . . . and then they would be able to write. Together. They would fuck and write and make things, it was all the same process. She would be so nice on that coverlet, and then all wrapped up in it later when he brought tea.

At three o'clock in the morning, David rang the night porter and asked him for coffee, sandwiches. He ate and drank quickly, very hungry, showered and made his bed. When he woke again it was time for breakfast and fully Saturday.

Monagh had baked them both biscuits.

'You can have another. There's no one else to eat them but me.'

'Thanks, they're very nice.'

She allowed herself a smile and crossed her legs with a nylon hiss.

'No need to sound quite so surprised.'

And Monagh grinned again, clattering the spoon as she put down her cup. She smoothed the grey woollen dress taut over her lap and glanced at the carpet, then the walls. When she flicked a hand through her hair, David caught a snatch of her perfume, clean skin and scented soap.

'Well, David, it's time to be very serious. I have something to show you, come on.'

Her tension seemed to melt as she moved for the door, pulling David up from the sofa by his hand. She tugged him behind her, out along the passageway, and he felt a heavy pulse start in his throat, felt his breath race, felt her fingers on his palm.

Monagh opened the furthest door and left him to drift in behind her. On the clean wood of her table, there was a narrow stack of foolscap sheets. She scooped it up and held it out towards him, eyes terribly blue, lips parting.

'How much will you give me for it? You win, you get first refusal. What am I bid?'

'I'm . . . Monagh. I . . . what do you mean?'

She smiled and dipped her head a touch to the side.

'David, it's what you were looking for; it's why you're here. I thought somebody would come, eventually. Silly things you think of when there's times on your hands. Please don't misunderstand me, David, I've given this up, I have no interest in this. But I did think, if I was so popular, so highly regarded -- you said it yourself -- I did think that someone might have wondered where I'd gone, if I was still writing, or if I had anything left behind unpublished.'

'Oh, I'm sure people wondered. I have. I've heard folk saying, really.'

'Well, it took a fucking while for you to ask me. You plural.'

She sighed, almost too softly to be heard.

'This is my last story. When I finished it, there wasn't any more. It stopped. That's the truth, I didn't stop it, it stopped itself. There were leftovers, attempts and rewrites and then nothing. I suppose my confidence had gone.'

'Your last story.'

'Yes. You can have it. I'll be perfectly honest with you, I need the money. Any money.'

'That's very, very . . . thank you. I'll have to be honest with you, too. I'm here to write an article about you, that is the only reason that I'm here. But as soon as I get home, I'll talk to people. They'll be very keen, I'm sure they will.'

Monagh returned the papers to the table without speaking, then sat with her back to the light. She would have sat like this when she was typing.

'So you'll hawk it round then, will you? Out with the begging bowl.'

'Look, it's my fault, you misunderstood me. This is my fault. I'll just leave you to think. Some more tea – I could make some. I'll do that. Yes.'

He turned and hoped to hear her crying as he walked along the hall. Crying would be good, a wee release. She'd prefer to do that privately and appreciate his tact.

'You see, David,'

She pulled his head round, made him stop before he knew what she had said.

'It does become quite important, after a while, that people ask you for your work. When you've been doing it for years, I mean for years; since I was your age; and the people who know how told you what a wonderful writer you are, you do just now and then, really want to be fucking asked.'

'Of course, I – '

'Don't say you understand. You do not understand. I'm not stupid, I worked very hard not to get my hopes up; just to write. But people say these things, you get reviews and you think you'll get work, at least something . . . I never had one offer of work in all those years. Not one.'

'Surely, there was something.'

'Never anything to do with writing – my writing. You end up doing nonsense; journalism, readings, anything, and folk think you're doing fine, they think you don't need to be asked. That's my problem, David, I never looked desperate enough.'

'But Monagh, if you were still able to work, if people liked what you did. Wasn't that enough?'

'No! It's not enough. I gave up too much for it ever to be enough. No one ever understood what I wrote, it never got any serious attention, it never changed anything. There just wasn't any point in doing it.'

'Monagh, please, come on and we'll go out. We'll have dinner.'

'Mr Reid, this is very sweet and I know you mean well. You seem a very nice young man, but please, just go away. You're too young to see this, you think you've got time to do better.'

'Oh for fuck's sake! You're so bloody self-obsessed. Do you know, you've talked about nobody else since I met you. Other writers are only there to be compared with you. Nobody else had it tough. You've got a house, you've got health, you've got your job, but you've got it tough. Why the hell should we all be waiting for every word you write? Who do you think you are? Why should your stories be able to change the world? If you want us all to jump whenever you have an idea, you should be a military dictator. Why write?

'You had it all there for you. You could get inside people's heads, change them by showing them things they'd never thought of, make them happy. You could plant the seed and maybe it wouldn't grow now, but it would do later. Only you've gone in the huff. You just don't want to play any more. You need to be asked, you say? Well who fucking doesn't. You have an obligation to us and you've chickened out.'

He found he was shouting, leaning over the table and starting to sweat.

'I'm sorry, I've . . . been offensive. I'll go.'

'Not at all. I apologise for letting you down, Mr Reid. I find one's idols are never quite up to scratch.'

'No, you haven't let me down. It just seems such a waste, Monagh. I mean a waste of you.'

'I don't think there's all that much of me left, David. Don't fret.'

They had tea in the living-room, very quietly, talking about Dublin and the places he should go to see. When she had fetched his hat and coat, Monagh sat beside him on the sofa.

'Do you think you'll write the article?'

'If you don't mind, I think I will. You know, it might make people ask you for work. It might not, though. I mean, I won't beg for you.'

'I know that. Look, take this, too.'

She had the manuscript in her hand.

'If anyone wants it, you can tell me. I refuse to be hopeful. But you might as well have it as not. That sounds very ungracious — I would like you to have it, David. There you are.'

Even out on the pavement, he could feel the pressure of her hand, through the paper. There was also the little weight of a kiss on his cheek.

'Bye, bye, David. No need to keep in touch. Unless something happens.'

And a doorstep kiss, an indecipherable gesture.

David caught a flight to Glasgow on Monday afternoon. Sunday had been too grey to make another week of Dublin seem bearable. He knew, if he stayed, he would end up calling her.

He walked out of Glasgow airport with his holdall unsearched, nothing he felt willing to declare. Somewhere between his shirts, he knew there was a sheaf of paper, just over a dozen pages, and he felt them tug his arm as he stepped. They carried a story called 'Warming My Hands and Telling Lies' which dealt with night-time disfigurements and invisible creatures called Industrialists. David worried it might be difficult to sell, but was happy to have it, as if he had suddenly met an old friend. A school friend. Only one thing had changed, now there was an introduction. Monagh must have added it later, or decided not to read it out one Friday afternoon, a very long time ago.

This story is as much as I can make it and must now speak for itself. Only you will know if it succeeds because I will stay here in the past and somewhere else.

My chosen title is a different case and does require additional explanation.

Once, out driving beside my second husband, I ran my fingers up his thigh. He asked me what I was doing.

'Just warming my hands.'

'Such lies.'

'Yes, I'm warming my hands and telling lies.'

You will recognise the relevant phrase.

As a year or two nudged past us, our relationship changed. My husband began to dislike me and then to hate. He hated my voice and my body, but perhaps most of all, he hated me to write.

'What are you doing?'

'What do you think?'

'Up there fucking writing all day, you'd be better off having a wank. Who do you think ever actually reads all that shite?'

'You don't object when it earns us money.'

'Remind me when that was, it's so long ago. I earn enough for both of us. Why don't you try retiring – you could take up being a wife.'

One day when I was asked what I was doing I shouted back, 'Warming my hands and telling lies.'

I don't know why these words occurred to me, only that they seemed entirely true. I sat and typed out fabrications, keeping my hands snug and supple on the little, black keys. That was all it came to, nothing more. Just warming my hands and telling lies.

LIKE A CITY IN THE SEA

'WELL, NEVER MIND about that – there was a pigeon on the underground.'

'But what happened? There are always pigeons everywhere. What did he say to you?'

'Almost nothing he hardly spoke. I mean this was a pigeon *on* the underground – going round on the Circle Line, just like a little drunk man in a grey vest. Staggering up and down the aisle.'

'All right, tell me about the pigeon.'

'It was on the Circle Line, walking up and down.'

'And?'

'That's all, really, I just thought it was worth mentioning. Everyone else was trying to ignore it, as if it *was* a little drunk man in a vest, you know?'

'Mm hm. What did he say?'

'Nothing you could put your finger on, but I knew what he meant.'

'Which was.'

'Whether you looked like my mother and whether we still fucked.'

There was a little quiver of sadness round her mouth

and then she gave him the look that meant he would have to say more. He didn't want to rehearse all the slimy details to her face, her unbearably patient eyes, so he moved to sit beside her on the sofa.

A room with three sofas, there was something excessive about that − about all of the furniture she had − but then all of the space she also had here just swallowed up whole sideboards as if they were biscuits. They could accommodate several pianos here, no trouble at all. As he sank down beside her, he thought of pianos and offered her the choice of looking out at the other two sofas, or sideways at him. He would be concentrating on the window.

'Well, go on then.'

She tapped the back of his hand and he leaned in a bit, catching a scent of her hair when he slipped his arm in under hers. She had the thinnest arms − each of them enough to break your heart.

'He talked about all of the usual stuff then plodded around for a while about what I do and how we met and did I know about your family − all that.'

'And what did you tell him?'

'What I always tell them − that most things are none of my business, but if you have chosen to tell me about them, then they're nobody else's, so there.'

He could hear her frowning.

'But I said it all very politely and smiled a lot.'

'Oh, dear, Sam.'

'What do you mean, "Oh dear, Sam"?'

'There's a way you have of smiling that looks hungry, rather than happy.'

'Well, that's just me, isn't it? Hungry rather than happy, that's me. I wouldn't be comfortable any other way. But the main thing he was interested in wasn't even to do with all that, everything always comes round to how many years you are older than me and how different we are. The Odd Couple – isn't it remarkable that we manage to stay together when there are 'fifteen or twenty years between us.'

'More like thirty years.'

'Yes, I told him that and he gave me one of those old-fashioned looks you'd remember from when you were young. Everyone knows it's nearly thirty, but he wanted to give the impression that he wouldn't believe it until he'd heard it straight from one of us. If you move across here more, you can see right into Number Thirty-Five – they've put their lights on. Mr Numberthirtyfive is having his first whisky and soda. Swallow, swallow, swallow – Good evening, world. He must have an awfully hard life. What does he do?'

She came in neat against his hip.

'Makes money.'

'Well of course, or he wouldn't live here, but what does he really do?'

'No idea. But that's his second whisky. Look at the way he's walking.'

'I bow to your superior knowledge of movement.'

He smoothed a little tug of hair back behind her ear and kissed the naked cheek beneath.

'How's Mum, then?'

'Mum's fine. How's Dad?'

'No complaints, not really. I'm sorry I ran away this afternoon, but I had to get off by myself for a while. Sometimes I'm better out than in.'

'Like wind.'

'If you must be romantic about it, yes, I suppose so.' He tried out the sound of it. 'I remember that Helen once told me I was like wind. I naturally reminded her that she was the one who was lighter than air. Yes, that seems fine.'

'Maybe you could suggest it as the title for the pro-gramme.'

'I will – "Helen Carlisle – Like the Wind. Like Having the Wind – Helen Carlisle." Or perhaps we could change it to "Like Indigestion". We wouldn't want to offend people, would we. What do you think?'

' "The Dancing Old Fart" would be better.'

'Perfect. Let's not talk about it any more. It annoys me, they annoy me. Let's have a nap.'

'I'm not sleepy.'

'Then I'm going to do this and this and have my own little doze, just here.' He stretched himself out with the back of his head just rested between the curves of her thighs, very supported, and nuzzled the side of his face against her belly. 'Mmm, smells like apple pie and roses, Mum.'

'Not sardines on toast, Dad?'

'Ooh, you are a one. Still, no point in not getting the full use of every settee. Wake me when it's supper-time.'

He didn't think about the crew until they had already arrived again the following morning. When he looked down out of the kitchen window, a man in an anorak was pressing a pale grey tripod into the slippery grass. There would be complaints about that from the Garden Committee — 'There shall be no use of tripods or other photographic supports to the detriment of lawns or other surfaces'. Not that the Court wouldn't love it, all the same. The district hadn't hosted a decent interview in months — nothing even faintly exotic to take for granted, not a parliamentary love-nest, not a film crew, not even a bomb.

Down on the lawn, the tripod was misbehaving. The fixing of one leg seemed automatically to loosen the other two and Anorak finally left the struggle and began to shuffle a darker green track across the misted turf, a boxy camera snugged between his ear and shoulder. The sound man was smoking a cigarette into the dusting rain. Nothing too much happening yet.

Sam tapped the window as he filled the kettle and smiled when Anorak waved up. The sound man never seemed to notice noises — not unless he wanted them for something.

Helen was reading a magazine when he went in to wake her. He'd wanted her to rest. Nobody realised how tiring all this was for her. She didn't tell them and they didn't have the wit to guess, because she could make any activity appear to involve no effort. She was born to be that way – no visible effort. Which didn't mean she didn't work, didn't mean he hadn't felt the difference in her muscles every night since this started. Sometimes she would tremble, caught in an extended movement, no room to be anything other than visibly weak.

Perhaps he just didn't like Twyford, the director. Maybe it was only ill-feeling that made him think the overall intention of the exercise was to ease Helen just a little more quickly on her way. The final documentary would be made, the old dancer in her kitchen, buying a magazine, pacing nostalgic sprung flooring in some god-forsaken hall and then she could die neatly, sufficiently immortalised. They were carving her memorial around her, already bending tiny incidents into myth. Sam had watched Twyford yesterday – the illustrious Ben Twyford – thinking himself into sparkling-eyed silence while Helen mashed out tinned sardines on to Rudolf's dish. The cat had sensibly boycotted the whole touching affair and the room was diving steadily towards some kind of scaley epitaph, Twyford chewed at his lip, his eyes reeling back and forward over a moment of senile fondness for a possibly imagined feline. He had sardine eyes.

Sam drew the blind up gently and let the grass and the daffodils in.

'Morning Mum. I thought you were having a late lie in.'

'Couldn't sleep, Dad. It's all the thrill of the filming. Last chance to shine.'

'Oooh, you are a card, Mum. You know you're used to it, really.'

'Not any more.'

He felt the depth of the carpet muffling underneath him as he came over to the bed. Funny how bedroom carpets always seemed the softest, he supposed it must be lack of wear.

'Don't be silly, you always shine. Like a film star, look at her − just awake and perfect hair, you wouldn't think she'd slept in it at all. Some people are lucky.'

She pursed her lips, disapproving and pleased. 'Sssh.'

'Show me something.'

Now her face cleared, almost emptied, except for the eyes. There was a tick of wariness there, or the fear of a future hurt.

'Go on.' It was important that he held her gaze while she rolled back the quilt. She had to be sure that he loved her from the inside out before he could break away and look at her powder pearl skin, the skinny girl limbs. He knew her all over − sometimes taut, like a teenage endurance runner, or suddenly damp, malleable as a new calf, all long bones and soft blinking. Time had finally breeched her lines, making her translucent and even more of what she had been always, the woman who was more air than substance. One morning she would be nothing at all, he knew it.

'That's Helen.' He winced at the clumsiness of his voice.

'What's left of her.'

'Now, now, Mum. Don't be morbid. Not when you can't see what I see. I would tell you if you weren't still beautiful.'

'Fibber.'

'Suit yourself. They want to have you walking in the garden, gliding through the spring bulbs, glimmers of light through the daffodils bending at your heels. Something like that. I don't think you should – it's raining.'

'I'm waterproof, Dad. Not a cripple yet.'

'I was only saying you might be miserable. You know how they make you stand about. See how you feel when you've had your bath, it's running.'

'Thank you, Dad. You're a lamb.

In the end she pleased them and went out to the garden. The rain was too insubstantial to show up on film. Only she would know she was wet which made it oddly all right. Sam went for another walk in the fine, washing morning. He'd been walking a lot lately, getting out of the way, out of any trouble he might cause.

He took an easy ten minutes, padding along clean streets of pastel and cream Victorian iced dollhouse buildings. It

was quiet here and smelled very faintly of spring, wet
brickwork and new paint. A young woman with casually
mountainous hair overtook him, a tiny dog squeezed
backwards under her arm like a miniature set of sniffling
bagpipes. He watched the wink and fall of the gold inlay
at the back of her heels and wondered how long her
shoes would last. They were more like carpet slippers,
belligerently delicate, a wonderful little proof that walking
and pavements need no longer be a part of life. Then he
was turning and fitting himself to the flow of the main
street, a slow burst of pedestrians from the underground.

Because it always made him feel uneasy to be here, he
ducked into a cafe for an early lunch. Three men sat round
a table at the back, all wearing hair unsuitable for countries
with weather.

'Have you seen the menu?'

He managed a hungry smile for the waitress.

'Yes, could I have the shepherd's pie?'

He would always say it that way – never 'I would like'
or 'I want', but 'could I have'. As if one day he would be
told that the shepherd's pie was too good for him, that
he shouldn't be there, that he couldn't have anything, go
away.

'The shepherd's pie is really lovely today.'

Which made him instantly feel disproportionately wise.
Without help, he had chosen the one dish on the menu
that was really lovely today. He knew that, when he paid
for his meal, another girl with assured hands and confident

eyes would ask him how his shepherd's pie was and he would tell her it was really lovely today. The girls and meals and restaurants were interchangeable, but everything would always be really lovely and today.

He smoothed down his moustache with the ball of his thumb and felt a real smile coming. There must be some Calvinist in him that he couldn't just enjoy this. Down in the blackened stump of a soul he imagined for himself, there must be something that longed to be uncomfortable. He should plunge into this whole whinnying gush of a city, watching it consuming and creating unsustainably, gleaming and floating on and on, blatantly unscathed for the simple reason that this all was so impossibly, wastefully, triumphally and enormously stupid that no one could even grasp enough of it to be angry.

He was angry, though. Even the nice steely blue they had managed for the sky outside made him angry. Today's walk wasn't going to calm him. He would stamp home, giving the man who sold the paper for the homeless too much money and offending him, being charitable and guilty and of no use.

'Well then, Sam. I just want to put something on film from what we discussed yesterday. Is that all right?'

Twyford gave him a paternal smile and crossed his legs with girlish ease. Sam found himself wishing that Twyford was gay – his affectation might have seemed likeable if it could have come from something human, something vulnerable. Or perhaps not.

'Is that all right?' The smile had been adjusted to brotherly but concerned.

'Yes, that's fine. Whatever you like.'

'Feel free to smoke, if you're nervous.'

'I don't smoke.'

'Down to business, then.'

If Sam had thought, he would have turned the radiators off, the lights were making the room almost unbearably hot. In the tropical conditions, Twyford seemed to swell and bray. His questions circled in and in, a hunting flicker in his fishy stare.

'It certainly seems odd. Helen Carlisle, of the shipping Carlisles, finishing school and then ballet school, an astonishing career, and you – a painter, you might say a rather minor painter, a socialist realist from a Liverpool Irish family.'

'We both had fathers in ships. One way or another – you know?'

'You met in London?'

So he wanted the whole deal, all the unexplainable business of how they met. Sam knew what always seemed miraculous to him would sound like self-interest to Twyford. He felt his voice lose its definition slowly, vowels wavering.

'It's such an old story. It was luck, that's all. Luck I

was working down here, or not working down here and a mate of mine had a job at the theatre where Helen was performing. That was the last season she danced, working with Bently as choreographer and partner, he was a youngster then – not ballet, new dance, very experimental in one way or another – I wouldn't have gone otherwise. And there I was in the stalls and there she was on the stage. That was that.'

'So simple?'

Even with Twyford watching, even with the black box eye of the camera watching, Sam was moving away to the first curve Helen had made in the air that evening. It had felt like an embrace, a woman in her forties, flinging her soul out to a younger, somehow less alive, man – matching his bursts of effort with something much slower; a huge, delicate power.

Every performance Sam could beg or buy a seat for, he'd been there, like an idiot. Like a mascot. Daft. And even then, he'd felt something slipping away from him. The plan he had made for his life, for all the important things he would do, it scattered, there wasn't even time to mourn it, until it was too long gone.

'Yes, it was very simple. My friend invited me to the last night party and pointed me out. I'd seen the show probably too many times, she was very nice about it, my faithful attendance.'

'And she invited you for tea?'

'That's her way of meeting people, she invites them for tea. Her health means she does it less often now, but that's still her way.'

'But you're the only one she married.'

'That's right. I don't know why that happened, but I'm glad it did. Maybe she remembered me because I didn't fit in. I was wearing several other people's clothes. I didn't have the kind of wardrobe you needed to have tea with ballet dancers in.'

As he'd left, Helen had held him back, her hand very firm around his, her mouth very close to his. She had told him, 'If you were a puppy, I couldn't take you in. Just look at the size of your feet. You'd have eaten me out of house and home, before you grew into them.'

Then she had dipped away from him a little, snatched a glance at his face and blushed which of course made him blush, too.

'I'm sorry, that was a silly thing to say.'

'No. No, it wasn't silly. But I won't grow any bigger, my wisdom teeth are through. I'm just not built in proportion to my shoe size.'

That had made her giggle and pat at the small of his back. Sam hoped Twyford had filmed Helen's giggle, her laugh, her smile. That would be something valuable. Sam tried to focus again on the prying little voice. It sounded like toothache.

'I'm sure. And your painting?'

'I don't do it any more. I still work now and then for myself, but I don't paint for other people. I have nothing I want to say – no, I have nothing I am able to say. I stay here with Helen and keep the place tidy, do the shopping, that kind of thing.'

'You look after Helen.'

'Helen looks after herself. And she keeps me – I'm a kept man. Don't know what Mam would have thought of that.'

'But as she gets older . . .'

'Oh, I suppose things will change, I don't know. In the end I'll go back to painting.'

'Really?'

'Yes. When she dies, I'll paint.'

'I beg your pardon?'

'I said, when she dies, I'll paint. This place will become mine, although I don't know if I'll stay here, and I'll paint. Something like that.'

'Some people might find that rather mercenary.'

'That would be their right. I find it rather necessary. Every day I think of Helen dying and of what I will do when she does and that makes it possible to stay here without being frightened. I couldn't wake up every morning afraid of being surprised by her death. I appreciate the time I have with her and I try to keep it real.'

Twyford failed to raise any suitable smile.

'When I saw her first, I knew, you see – from my throat to the pit of my stomach and down the insides of my arms, like that, I could feel it — I knew something had happened. It was out of my hands — I would stay with her until she died and that would be the best way I could occupy my time. Nothing else was possible any more. After this, I'll do something else until I die and that may mean I paint, or sell papers, or devote my life to saving endangered donkeys. More and more, I think that the dying will be the important thing — not what I do at all. Do you ever think that?'

'I'm not sure I know what you mean.'

'Well, I look out of the window behind you there, for instance. Lovely red brick and white plaster or whatever the hell it is, very pretty, very perfect — the leaded windows facing out on it all and our awfully nice, well-regulated garden down below. And it's all been here for — what — a hundred years, a bit more. But I see all that and it seems it must have been there forever — forever and flawless — not an expression of power, or wealth, but a power in itself. After a while I'll start to feel a little bit crazy, I'll dream about blowing things up, just to prove it's possible to get some movement here, to make it real and decaying like the people. I mean I wouldn't bomb the people, just the place. You won't use that bit, will you?'

'Some viewers might find it offensive.'

'I suppose so. In any case, I mainly think about dry rot, wet rot, woodworm, subsidence — the slow kinds of explosion. I mean, people are so good at ignoring things here, they don't even really notice the bombs any more

— they're just something else nasty on the street. Inconvenient. Even I believe this is all invulnerable now. Guy Fawkes didn't change it, Hitler didn't change it, nor will I. It's an island in an island here, we make it like that in our heads. I know I do. Now the only way I can relax and live with myself is to think that changes will happen more slowly than I can see. What I find most important is that thinking of death — Helen's and mine — makes it quite possible to be alive. I get a sense of perspective this way and I don't worry so much. It doesn't drive me crazy to be here and not be able to do anything much about anything. Paint or don't paint, dance or don't dance, film or don't film — it doesn't matter, does it?'

That sounded final enough to Sam, but Twyford rallied for one last lunge at Sam's Socialist principles, his artist's need to communicate and lead the way. Sam could only presume he didn't have these things any more because nothing Twyford said seemed to even touch them. Inside, he felt peculiarly peaceful.

'You've never thought of leaving; the age difference, there's never been a strain?'

One late jab.

'No, Ben. I've never thought of anything like that. If you knew Helen, you wouldn't either.'

'Well, thanks, Sam. I don't know how much of that we'll be able to use. It will certainly give us another perspective on Helen, but she will always be in the focus.'

'That's always fine with me.'

Twyford's eyes shut down and he patted his jacket pockets for the lighter he had left on the arm of the chair.

Sam went into the bathroom, locked the door and filled the sink with sour London water. He pressed his face down through the cold thick of it until his eyes began to prickle and his ears roared and then he gulped back and up, taking in long, aching gasps of air. His reflection blinked and dripped, its nose running, then smiled and sank to the water again. This time the overflow splashed his feet. When he was finished he would put on dry clothes and clear up the mess, but for now he was washing his brains and he didn't know a way to do that and be tidy.

'Well, Dad, they've gone, then.'

'No more attention.'

'All for the best, Dad. It would have gone to our heads.'

'There would have been no talking to us. Still, we'd better watch it – it'll prove we're real. Nothing like being on the telly to make you real.'

'He's doing something in Surbiton next. Or Serbia, one or the other.'

'Wouldn't be Serbia, Mum. Very messy and nasty out there. Who would want to do with that?'

They would sit on the red sofa and watch Mr Number-thirty-five drink his whiskies and talk about the filming tonight. That would get it out and over with, no need to mention it again. Sam kissed her throat and felt the movement of her voice.

'Is it next month, we're on, Dad?'

'The one after.'

'Think we'll still be here then?'

He slipped his arms around her, his palms against her ribs, holding her breath.

'I wasn't thinking of leaving. Were you going somewhere, Mum?'

'I'm not sure. Such funny things happen, Dad. I never know.'

'Nice to be here for the show, eh? Early to bed and keep healthy, we'll probably both be here.'

'Then maybe we'll watch it together, then.'

'Yes, Mum, we'll do that.'

She smoothed his cheek, close and slow so that he could hear her touch, the faintly electric disturbance of muscle and finger joints, the sound of her mechanism working.

Mixing With The Folks Back Home

My dear daughter,

I can imagine you may have been wondering why I
never did explain about you and your father and why it
is that you are not related.

We spoke about it one time before, I know, and I said
— the same as always — that another time would be more
suitable. Now the days and the years have gone by and
that suitable time never has come along which is why I
decided to write you and get this done.

'You want this thing done, then go right ahead and do
it, get it done.' That's what your father says and I agree
with him.

Well, this all happened a long time ago and a long way
from you and me both. I was in another state. The State
of Matrimony.

No. That was a joke. But I was married, sure enough,
and living in a little place far away from here, but pretty
much the same. We had more frogs there, is all. A lot of
years, I've thought about it and that's the only difference
I can come up with. More frogs and maybe less folks

which is about the way I like it. You know I never was the social butterfly type.

One summer I was the age you are now, or darn close to it, and it seemed like the whole world was fixing to lay down and die. Everywhere you looked, nothing but yellow dust and white dust and the husks of bugs and now and then some unfortunate critter, flat down and dried up and dead. I lifted a big old catfish once, right up out of the creek bed, didn't weigh more than a handful of leaves and so stiff and dry it snapped clean in two just like a week old piece of corn bread. Except it was a different shape and colour than corn bread, of course.

And there I was, in a little grey house that was nothing but dry and tight as an old skin. Used to rattle and snap and drumbeat all night and I can still hear the BANG it used to make out of even the littlest step. I should know, I only made the littlest steps then. I had a figure in those days, I was petite, and walking just as soft as ever I could because there was a baby in the house. That was you. My daughter.

I tiptoed across those rooms day and daily with the nice waist that you didn't spoil one bit, being such a tiny, bitty thing when you were born. Folks would get worried just looking at you, you were so small, but I didn't ever worry. I just loved you like my mother loved me and that did fine for both of us. We were company for each other.

Now you'll want me to tell you who else was in that place with us, or if we were there alone. Well a man called

Taylor Whitman was there, too, and he was a friend of my father's and he was also my husband. He would be what you would call your biological parent along with me.

Don't you worry, on his account, neither. He wasn't just as nice as your father is now, but he was good enough and I didn't know any better, not then.

Taylor Whitman was a quiet man who owned the hardware store and had a keen interest in frogs. He would chase a particular frog for miles, just to look at it, hear it sing. Course most times, he'd catch whichever one was nearest, cut off its legs with a little knife he had and throw it up for our dog, Buddy, to catch. Buddy had a keen interest in frogs, also.

Taylor Whitman was not handsome, but he was agreeable and could play fine Bluegrass banjo and sing simultaneously. He would sit out on the porch nights, drinking beer, listening to the bugs and singing. He was happy that way. Once he told me that good white folks had a duty to play the banjo, or it would get left to the jazz artists and negroes and those white trash, albino types up in the hills that you read about. I don't know if that was why he got so allfired happy, those nights, but he certainly did love that banjo.

There was one unfortunate thing about Taylor which neither of us guessed until after our marriage, because our courting was conducted very properly, with him being such a close friend of my father and, in any case, not inclined to be energetic with anything other than frogs. Taylor Whitman was allergic to my skin. Didn't matter what I did. If I washed or didn't wash or rubbed myself with who knew what kind of fancy preparation sent direct by mail, it didn't make no difference. I couldn't set a finger on him without his blistering up — cablooey — like an acid-burned bullfrog. It was a shame.

We were a close couple, all the same. I got into the habit of wearing gloves around the house and our intimate relations were assisted by kind of flannel all-over bodysuits that his mother ran up out of underwear and some additional pieces for the face and so forth. You see, there was a point to all that because Taylor Whitman had a place where he wasn't one tiny bit allergic. He would get almost amphibious about those times we could spend together with his mama's help. She even put a little needle-point embroidery around those important places where the flannel had to be left open which I thought was kind of cute but weird all the same, from somebody's mother and all.

Weird or not, almost every possible night we'd squeeze on into those suits, shuffle up and hug each other like we were fire-fighters or bee-keepers, or Lord knows what and Taylor Whitman's bitty eyes would be sparking through his bitty eye-holes and then we'd be off and under the sheets.

And those suits were hot, even without sheets. The summer I'm talking about, was just around the time I had decided those suits were too darn hot altogether. I would lie in the early morning, listening to Taylor Whitman's big old boots just busting the boards underneath him and hearing the dawn outside, already too hot and stiff and cracked to do anything more than sigh. I'd get a big blue feeling and pretend I was asleep until he'd gone, which was pretty easy when he couldn't see none of my face on account of the suit. And when he was gone I'd walk around that house bare naked with the blinds drawn, just to feel broke out and healthy a little. I had an idea that if the heat kept on a month longer, I'd wake up one morning boiled down to the bone.

I was tired all the time. Just to breathe was making me tired and it didn't seem my life would ever be any different from the way it was then. I would always be looking after Taylor Whitman and looking after his big, dry house and tending to his frogs and his mother's sleeper suits. You were the only brightness in my life, I can tell you. I would purely live to sit out by the back door with you and see what new things you'd thought of to do, all fresh there under the shade and the loving sun.

You were just kind of accomplished in smiling when a beat-up, green station wagon pulled in back of the house and a man wearing coveralls and sneakers climbed out. He stood with his arms crossed, real snug, and smiled right over at you and me, like he was throwing us a flower. Then waved his hand and he said, 'Good morning, Mrs Whitman, ma'am. Your husband told me I should

come right over, take a look at the land for those new
frog pens he'd been planning. Hope I don't disturb you
none. Oh my, but that's a lovely child. What is her name?'

He knew you were a girl right off from the start and I
wasn't used to menfolk taking much of an interest in
children that weren't of their own making, leave alone
recognising what kind they were, so I must say was glad
to have the acquaintance of this man who ambulated clean
up the path, shook my hand, real gentle, and told me
what he was called.

'Robert McConnerey Coons, Ma'am, Robert McConnerey Coons. And I am most delighted to meet you.'

As the weeks went by, I grew used to the visits from the
station wagon and the neat noises there would be around
the house and outside from Robert McConnerey Coons
tapping and sawing and hammering, setting things right.
Mr Coons himself didn't make no noise at all. He was
lighter on his feet than I was, only his feet was bigger,
naturally.

He finished the frog pens in double quick time and they
looked as pretty as a line of doll's houses, all painted up.
but then there was the fence to mend and things wrong
with windows and the bug screens and the roof. It was a
wonder the house hadn't just split right open one night,
like an overwatered melon, and killed us all stone dead.
But Robert McConnerey Coons got everything fixed –
he was downright indispensable.

'You can call me Bob, if you like. Most folks do.'

'Well, you can call me Irma Jean, Bob.'

'Why, is that your name, Irma Jean?'

'Yes, it is, Bob.'

'That's one bee-ootiful name. Irma Jean.'

Taylor Whitman seemed to like Bob just as much as I did. The store ran much better when Bob was helping out. He had a way of talking to people that set them entirely at ease and he could have made a sow buy belly pork and like it. And it was a wonder, how much he seemed to do in a day.

'Well, I just work the way I feel I should, Irma Jean. That's all. My Papa, he never did have the trick of doing anything for long and finally he died with no money and no home to speak of and it was a bad and shameful business altogether. I never knew my Mama, see – so he was all the folks I had.'

'I'm sorry, Bob.'

'Thank you, but there's no need. I don't mind it now. I just feel that being an orphan and all, I should show men and women who are born with a bad start in life that they can turn out just fine, all it takes is application – get up and go.'

'There should be more people like you, Bob.'

'Oh, I don't know about that. But I do know the world sorely needs more doing and less belly-aching. Nobody owes me a living, I make my own.'

He did, too. Taylor Whitman would come in, almost every day and tell me something good that Bob had done. He would go anywhere in town, if somebody happened to mention they had a child's swing needed fixing or an automobile wouldn't start, any little troublesome thing. He helped out in the store and round the town, built our house all over again from the ground up and still had time for his own work. Taylor Whitman said Bob was always buying a new axe-head, or a saw blade, or a special knife. It sort of made it all come together when Bob happened by one night with his fiddle and started up playing, sweet as maple, alongside Taylor Whitman, both of them pulling on bottled beer and making music in time with the bugs. That night, I fell asleep with the sound of Bob's fiddle still hopping and sliding out over the rosebud archway he helped me plant. And all the way inside of me, I had the happiest feeling I'd ever know, like a little golden frog, dancing under my heart.

Then, one day Taylor Whitman went out of town to see a man upstate about some lizard traps. He left Bob to mind the store.

'Morning, Irma Jean.'

'Why, Bob, you should be back in town, filling in for Taylor Whitman.'

He'd surprised me, I have to say. Bob surely did sneak on those sneakers of his. All the way into the house and I never knew he was there until I felt him breathe, up close behind me. I'd of been scared, if he hadn't been smiling so nice.

'I'm sorry. I scare you?'

'No, Bob, not a bit.'

That was a lie on my part, but a nice one, so it didn't count. I've always said, it ain't *what* you do, it's your attitude while you do it that should count.

'I'm glad you weren't scared. You don't have nothing to be afraid of from me. I promise.'

'Well, thank you. What brings you here? Did Taylor Whitman have a message for me?'

'Not at all. I was out this way, doing some repairs for old Mr Haarman. I left a note at the store, say where I was. I won't be away long and it's always quiet in the mornings. I thought I'd stop by and tell you good morning, say how much I appreciated your hospitality, when I first come to town.'

'Thank you, Bob. That's very kind.'

'You been kind to me. I remember that. Better lock your door now, when I go. There's things happen, you know.'

I did know, too. Everyone had heard about it — there were folks dying. I won't go into details, because it was all a long time ago and there's no need to be specific. I think it's enough to say that drifters were showing up dead. A whole recreational vehicle full of Californian transient types were found in the woods by the Interstate. All dead. It was kind of weird, because nobody knew why so many folks were being killed – and they were killed for sure, none of them died any way you could have called natural. But nobody could get too riled up about it, neither, because none of the dead folks was anybody you could put a name to. We didn't know them and we didn't know anyone that did. They just weren't the kind you'd call necessary.

Leastways, that's how it seemed to me. It was only Taylor Whitman made me think it could have the least thing to do with us.

'Irma Jean Whitman?'

'Yes, Taylor Whitman.'

'You been talking to that Bob Coons?'

'Not lately.'

Which was true. I hadn't seen him for a couple of days, but I did blush up a touch because I enjoyed Bob's company a tiny bit more than Taylor Whitman's, what with me and him being unable to touch and all.

'Well, don't you let him in the house no more, you hear?'

'Why ever not?'

'Because I tell you not.'

Taylor Whitman could be like that. Specially when he was short of frogs and the drought had just plain dried them up, by then. He had a man in Seattle mail him frogs, but they were all dead on arrival, didn't matter what he did.

So the next time Bob came by the house, I almost

opened up the door to him, because I'd forgotten what
Taylor Whitman done told me. Bob remembered,
though.

'No, Irma Jean. Don't you open that door. Hiya.'

That 'Hiya' was for you. He'd always pay you attention, no matter what.

'But, Bob, that's nonsense. Taylor Whitman just got a
wild hair about something, it's not to do with you.'

'Oh, it is, Irma Jean. It is to do with me. Come up by
the window and I'll tell you it all.'

So I moved on over by the window and opened it up
so I could look down at Bob. That window just smoothed
open — Bob'd done another good job there.

'Irma Jean, what did he tell you?'

Bob seemed kind of serious and was talking real low.

'Oh Bob, he didn't tell me nothing, only said I shouldn't
let you in the house. I said it was nonsense, but he
wouldn't listen.'

Bob stared down at his sneakers awhile, then drew in
a long breath.

'Well, I gotta be honest with you, Irma Jean. I ain't
honest too much, but you brought me to it. Taylor Whitman is right, kind of, you shouldn't let me in the house.'

'Well, why not?'

Bob messed around in the dirt with one of his feet and
then started up talking again, awful quiet now.

'Irma Jean, you know there's been folks dying? Last

month, it was nearly twenty men and women, all cut up
– pieces missing and, in several awful instances, no heads.'

'Twenty – that is a lot isn't it?'

'That's nearly one person every day, Irma Jean, if you
spaced them out even, and they die horrible. Why, if they
weren't tortured and heartlessly slaughtered way out of
town, no one would get any sleep. You know that?
Screams carry, that's what they're for.'

'I hadn't thought about it, Bob.'

'I'm glad, Irma Jean, that proves you're a good person,
like I always thought. Thing is, all of these bodies were
killed with different sharp objects – sometimes a knife
and a chisel, or a saw blade, or an axe. An axe is used
very often, one way or another. Now does that make you
think of anything?'

'Well, I suppose it's kinder that way, than killing them
with a blunt object – I always thought that sounded kind
of drawn-out and clumsy when you read about it in the
papers.'

'Well, bless your heart, that's a very considerate
thought. But I'm afraid, your husband doesn't have your
way of thinking.'

'What do you mean, Bob?'

Bob jumped up and rested his chin over the window,
so he was kind of there in the room and he give me such
a long, soft look.

'Irma Jean, Taylor Whitman thinks I'm the one doing
it. All of that perverse and conscienceless butchery.'

'Oh, Bob – he's only fooling. Taylor Whitman has an odd sense of humour, I always say it's the time he spends with things that croak, spoils him for regular conversation.'

'You have a lovely soul, Irma Jean, but this is serious. Taylor Whitman owns the hardware store, he's sold me all types of sharp object over these months and he's remembered each and every one. An awful lot of those objects have turned up at the crime scenes – even the long nails and the wire.'

'But you didn't do all those things, did you? Bob?'

Bob give a tiny cough and blinked. Slow.

'Would you turn me in if I had?'

'Of course not, you ain't ever done no one here any harm. Everybody round here likes you. They would say the same. Sometimes Taylor Whitman's opinions just get me fit to be tied. I am sorry if he has offended you.'

'That's all real good to know, Irma Jean. I have to be going now. You take especial care, I mean that. Bye.'

He dropped back down to the dirt and walked away, didn't say another word. Now I heard not a thing more about Robert McConnerey Coons for a week or so and then one night Taylor Whitman said that Bob had to take a trip and see his mother who was sick up in Alaska. He wouldn't be around for a while. I knew that just wasn't true because Bob was a orphan and that we must of hurt Bob somehow and made him leave, so that blue feeling come over me again and I went to bed early without my suit. Taylor Whitman must of felt bad, too, because he was up pretty much the whole night, fooling with his banjo and listening to how lonesome it could sound without Bob, playing up alongside of it.

The whole town missed Bob. You couldn't walk down the street without someone asking if he would be gone long, if he was coming back. There were still bodies turning up in the woods or out at the lake — all over the state — but mostly we didn't talk about that, we wondered about how Bob was getting along. That's the way the Good Lord made us, we care about people, even strangers once we get to know them. One woman — Bob fixed her daughter's wooden arm — she was all for driving clean up to Alaska with herbal remedies she'd cooked up to cure his mother. She would of done it, too, only the Deputy knows she can't really drive an automobile and won't let her go outside of town, case she gets in trouble.

About this time Taylor Whitman had himself a scheme to build a snake pit which I was worried about because of you maybe falling in it, or the snakes maybe getting loose, but it wasn't working out anyway because he didn't know how to dig it right and it just fell in all the time, without Bob to help. In the end, even he had to say, 'I surely wish Bob was here, he'd get this done in a minute, I know.'

Now you remember how I always used to tell you that wishes come true? Well, this is when I learned that. I don't know how much Taylor Whitman's wishes counted for, but I'd been wishing Bob would come back, ever since

he left and I'm not ashamed to say it. Each morning, I'd
walk about behind my drawn down blinds and think of
the way he stood that first morning in those neat, dusty
red coveralls, just looking at you and me. I even took to
leaving my doors unlocked, as if that would seem more
welcoming, if he ever did show up again.

Naturally, when Taylor Whitman turned in for the
night, he'd lock all the doors to keep us safe until morning
time. Least that's what he thought and so did I, until I
woke up while it was still dark and saw Bob standing
there at the end of the bed. He snuck up alongside of me
and whispered, 'I had the other keys for your new locks.
Hope you don't mind.'

I was getting used to how dark it still was in the room
and I could see him bite his lip a little and seem to think
of something. Then I went clean back to sleep, awful
sudden.

When I woke up, there was sunlight, shining in through
the eyeholes of my suit and I was not in a comfortable
position.

You know what had happened?

Bob had taken Taylor Whitman and me out of the
house, knocked unconscious, and he had put us down in
the hole that was waiting to be Taylor Whitman's snake
pit. I found that impolite, to say the least, and I didn't
waste any time in telling that old boy, Robert McConnerey Coons just what I thought of him when he happened
by with his spade.

'Robert McConnerey Coons, just what exactly do you think you're doing?'

'Well, Irma Jean, I was going to bury you. Why? You worried about your daughter? She's just fine. I'll see she gets taken care of, don't you worry a bit.'

That was a weight off of my mind, but Bob still had me disappointed. Don't you think otherwise.

'Don't worry? What sort of fool thing is that to say to someone in a snake pit?' Which was a slight exaggeration, as you know, what with the pit being hardly finished, but I was mad and felt my remark was justified at the time. 'Why shouldn't we worry? Did we ask to be buried alive?'

'Not exactly, no. But I really can't have people knowing what I do. Taylor Whitman there, he knows about the tools I bought and you know I ain't got no Mama up in Alaska. I stayed around, hoping you'd both keep quiet, but then I just got awful nervous. I like my freedom, Irma Jean, and I love life. They kill people who kill people in this state and I would not enjoy that.'

'Bob, what you do in your own time is nobody's business but your own and people round here believe in letting what's private stay that way. You should know that. Your behaviour this morning is plain uncivilised.'

'I'm sorry, Ma'am. But it don't look to me like I have any choice.'

'I know and we all make mistakes when we're being hasty. I can appreciate your predicament. Now how about you pull me up out of this hole and I'll fix us some breakfast? Then we can talk, work something out, don't involve so much death and unpleasantness.'

Bob didn't seem too sure about that, but I gave him my biggest Sunday morning smile and he reached down his hand, lifted me up, real easy. He was a very strong person, I'd guessed that.

I was hoping that some home cooking and coffee would calm Bob down — even if coffee is a stimulant. He did seem to settle some and even let me go change out of my sleeper suit, because I was walking that pit dirt all through the house, the mess it had got into.

Through the bedroom window as I fixed myself up, I could see Taylor Whitman's hands, scrabbling at the dirt round the edge of the hole. He was OK and on his way out to see what in hell was going on. I could tell he was mad, just from looking at his fingertips.

Back in the kitchen, Bob was almost through with his ham and eggs, dabbing at his mouth very particularly with a napkin. I like a neat man.

'Bob, how you feel now? You want some biscuits?'

'I'm just fine, Irma Jean, thank you. I knew you'd be an excellent cook. You'd better come along with me now, I have to get on. Where'd I put that spade, you remember?'

'Down by the pit, Bob, but things don't have to be this way. You can change.'

'I don't want to change. I like the way I am.'

'Do you really, Bob?'

'Yes ma'am, I surely do.'

I stared him in the eye for that answer and he stared back, real steady and sincere and I got to thinking that I liked him the way he was, too. No argument about it. So I took a step closer and leaned in to say, 'Then how about you and me go down to the pit, Bob. Taylor Whitman ain't dead yet and he's trying real hard to get out.'

Bob gave me a smile then, shone up the room. I can recall thinking how it seemed to sparkle with the sun off of the cream jug in just the sweetest way.

'Thank you for letting me know that, Irma Jean. You know why it is, he's still alive? You took away my concentration so much I did not hit him the way I should, you goshdarn delicate thing, you. You want to come outside?'

'If you'll hold my hand, Bob.'

'Why certainly I'll hold your hand. That, ma'am, would be a pleasure.'

It was very still out, but I could smell something a little like rain on the air, definitely a softness that hadn't been there in such a long while.

Down in the yard, Taylor Whitman was still scratching at the rim of the pit like a big old dog, cussing too. Bob squeezed my hand and whispered.

'What you think we should do, honey? He's kind of hard to get at down there and I won't use a gun, they're too noisy and no dang fun at all. Ain't got one.'

Well, Bob calling me 'honey' like that, just started the day off all over again, nice and fresh.

'Why don't we bury him, Bob?'

Bob turned and winked at me, 'That's what I was aiming for, Irma Jean, but he ain't dead yet.'

'But I think that's for the best, don't you?'

'Oh, honey, where you been hiding all of my life?'

Bob didn't say that too softly which set Taylor Whitman hollering like he was on fire or something so we had to bury him kind of quick and I didn't have any time to say good-bye. Still, after it was over, Bob told me to go set my ear down to the ground, see if I could hear something. Sure enough, Taylor Whitman was still belly-aching just a bit and stirring around so I shouted down into the earth that I would always remember him and thank you for our lovely daughter and I hoped it was appropriate for him to die kind of short of breath on a hot morning in his sleeper suit, because I had often dreamed of going out that way myself. If he said anything back I couldn't hear it.

After that, Bob and I washed up and drank some more coffee. We'd both had a kind of disturbed night so Bob took off his shoes and slept on the couch while I went back to bed. It must have been two or three hours later that the rains come.

The thunder was bowling and rushing itself all over the sky and over each of the little wood houses in our town and the drought aching fields and the snapping dry woods and our memorial silent garden and our sand-bellied yard where Taylor Whitman was buried and dead. All that disturbance just drifted sweet and easy over you, but it woke me and I lay under my sheet and nothing else, while the entire house let out one big, contented breath and then began to loosen up under whole loops and clatters and spouts of rain. I walked through to watch it fall against the windows, not even noticing Bob was there until he rose up from the couch and walked straight to me, put his arm round my waist while the lightning shone in his hair. His hand fluttered against me, near my hip and it seemed a mighty fine thing that his skin could be close up to mine. I considered that might happen quite often from then on.

Bob and I lived on at Taylor Whitman's house for almost a year and nobody seemed to bother too much that Taylor Whitman was gone. The town was glad that Bob was home and that was all. The only regret I hold about that time is how we had to have that dumb dog, Buddy, put to sleep. He was the only one seemed to miss Taylor Whitman and he would keep on digging up the dirt to get him back. Nearly made it, too.

We lived a good life and business at the store continued well, even if Bob did keep the stock kind of depleted on the sharp object side of things. Which brings me to the only difficulty Bob and I ever had with each other.

'Couldn't you stop it for a little while, darling?'

'What do you mean?'

'I mean the killing people thing. Don't you get tired of it, ever?'

'Not yet.'

'Lord knows, I wouldn't stand in the way of your interests, but won't you get in trouble one day? I'd hate to lose you.'

'Well, I'd hate that, too. As it happens, folks are getting awful cautious, round here. Suspicious, too. There ain't the visitors passing through like there used to be. I'm running out of strangers I can kill and I'd just hate to have to start up and kill folks we knew.'

'Well, I should hope so. That would be just like murder, wouldn't it? But what do we do about this, Bob? It's getting to be a problem. You're practically emptying the state.'

'I know and I've thought about it. The only thing to do is just to up and move away to someplace else. I know you like it here and I do too, but it could be we have to sell up and get on the road.'

Now I didn't want to leave the town where I'd been born one little bit and the idea of it made me very blue. I even got mad about it, which I never did with Bob as a rule.

'Robert McConnerey Coons, I don't see why you and your precious serial killing should mean I have to be uprooted from every darn thing I know. That doesn't seem fair to me.'

'We'd go someplace nice, I promise.'

'And then what? We'd just have to move out again when you'd cleaned up all the drifters and loafers and welfare types. I am not a travelling salesman, I need to be settled in my life. I have a daughter and attractive break-ables to think of.'

'But I don't know what to do, honey.'

'What if I cut *your* arms off with an electric saw, break your legs and leave you in the woods all night before I kill you? Would that set you thinking?'

'How'd you know about that?'

'I read the papers. And all I see there is you having fun and not thinking of your family one bit. We *are* your family now, you know.'

The thought of having a family all of his own seemed to knock the air clean out of Bob and, before I knew it, he was holding on to my hand and crying worse than Taylor Whitman had during his interment.

'I'm sorry you had to read that. If there's one thing I hate it's the morbid interest in violent crime, as evidenced by certain elements in the media. But I don't know what to do, honey. I can't stop. I can take a week out, even two, but then I need to get back to killing. I need to hear those noises they make. I need them fresh.'

'Well, consarnit, why can't you buy a tape-recorder like any normal person would?'

I was in a tough mood that day, I'd about had enough, washing all that blood and bone out of his things — it was worse than the frogs.

'I tried it, Irma Jean. But I need the variety of sound. It's not the killing I like, not really, it's just that every one of them says different things, you know? They all beg and plead and whimper and shout in individual little ways – that's a precious thing to me, it gives me a kind of faith in each person's unique humanity, even in this cruel old world of mass production and drive-in funeral homes.'

'Robert McConnerey Coons, I'll move with you once and it's got to be a nice, clean-living town we go to. But I only move once, mind, you don't sort this out, we're in for stormy weather, you and me.'

I found I was a much more forthright woman since I'd stomped down the earth over Taylor Whitman. I'd realised, you can do that to a husband, or anybody else, any time you like.

So we lifted up Taylor Whitman, buried him again in the woods, to save any inconvenience for the next owners of his house and we made the move to the home that you were raised in, the home where I'm writing this.

I'm sitting in the kitchen while your father is out in the woodshed, if you want to know. You will have guessed by now that Bob is your real father. We changed his name to Buddy when we got here, after Taylor Whitman's dog. The name Elwood we took from another couple that your father met up with one night on the journey north – I never saw them, but they sounded real nice.

How come we've stayed here so long and happy and kept your life so undisturbed by your Papa's homicidal tendencies?

Technology – that was the answer. Technology.

I don't mind admitting, things were getting about as out of hand as they could get with your Papa. He got the house fixed up and had a job over at the garage, but as soon as he got the garden in shape, he was off serial killing again. I was happy because it made him happy and he come home with money from people he had dealt with now and then which helped to keep us comfortable and put you through school, but our happiness was founded on sand, as my Mama would have said. It was only a matter of time before something unpleasant occurred.

Then I was sitting home, watching TV, and a genuine miracle came to pass. I couldn't wait to tell your father when he come in. It was another late night for him and I was so full up with the news that I sat on the edge of the tub while he scrubbed the blood out of his ears, didn't wait for him to come downstairs.

'Buddy, it's happened. I've found a way out.'

'What's that, hon? You found what? Could you burn that, by the way, I don't think it'll wash.'

'Oh, hush up and listen some, boy. You don't have to do this any more. I found a way you can stop.'

'Irma Jean, we've been through all this a hundred times.'

'But it's different now, listen.'

And I told him how they'd come up with machines, could take any noise at all and make it higher or lower or changed altogether, just mix it around any way you liked. What he had to do was record the sounds he got off of maybe eight or ten more people and he'd never have to kill a fresh one again. We had plenty of money saved by then, we could go right out and buy what we needed, put it in the woodshed, where he kept all those sharp objects of his.

Your Papa weren't too sure about it at first, but he come round to my way of thinking in the end and was very conscientious about collecting up every little noise and whisper those final few people let out. It happened he couldn't really let it go at ten and kind of eased the numbers up to fifteen but then I said that enough was enough.

He wound up with hours and hours of tape and what with Buddy being so practical-minded, it wasn't long before he was out in the woodshed almost every night with his itty-bitty earphones on, mixing it up to beat the band. We could be happy again.

Now I won't say your Papa has never caught another live one, but I'm too soft-hearted to say he shouldn't ever go out and have some fun. Once in a while for old time's sake ain't so bad and he always tapes every detail, so there's no waste involved.

Which pretty much wraps it up, sweetheart. I'll sign off now before your Father gets back. We both sincerely hope you're doing fine and will come see us whenever you can. We both of us miss you every day and think of you often as we know you think of us. Like your Papa says, 'Our kind of folks stay close, it doesn't matter what.' So our best wishes and prayers go along with this letter, as always. Pleasant dreams and good night.

NOW THAT YOU'RE BACK

AND BECAUSE SOMETIMES he no longer knew what to do, or how to be, he went up to the emptied church on the hill and simply looked out of the window for a while.

He supposed he might spend a good deal of time here, staring down at the grass barrelling and sinking over the old graves, the blue-green slopes beyond it turning suddenly into rocks and sea. His memory wasn't the best thing about him, but he was sure he had never seen a place like this. There was something impatient here about the sky, something with no space in it for men and an anger to swallow their works. The church had survived by becoming another stone among stones and setting its congregation safe underground. There were seven hundred years of them here, it said so on the plate fixed by the door.

Which he wished he'd never read because now he couldn't walk here without thinking of stamping down on to yards and yards of spent bone and compressed personality. There was no particular sense in his thinking that way because everywhere here must run just as deep and peculiar as everywhere else. He could tell that just by looking. Through the window there was nothing but dust in water, water in peat-turf, peat-turf on rock and bare rock dipped in naked air and hard against raw water and millions of atoms of millions of years of dust. A frightening peacefulness. No argument, it was old – dusts and rocks and waters were the oldest things possible, they were part of the planet and nothing he knew could be older than that, not really.

A thin breeze wavered between the stones of the wall and the little sheet of glass conserving the space where a window would once have been. He let the pressure of air wash against his face, skim over his hair and his eyelids and into his brain. Open his mouth and he could taste something slightly ocean and damp, just pushing fresh along his gums. Nice.

Rather than go straight inside when he came to the caravan, he turned down the track for the pool and began to skim stones. His first few efforts flew off numbly, crushing the surface into plumes and spidery disturbances that scampered up to the banks. A fluke attempt skipped twice over what seemed more and more like a thick dish of sky as he squinted at it, concentrating, trying to find a comfortable way to move his arms. He hadn't tried skimming anything in years – seemed like hundreds of years. He could not picture himself as the boy who did this once without thinking, good at throwing things.

He knew he should relax more with his swing, try to feel unobserved and not ridiculous. It wasn't as if he was doing harm, only playing to himself, by himself, that shouldn't make him feel so uneasy.

'Just like a human being, eh, Tom? See anything too lovely and you just have to start chucking stones. We've all got to make our mark.'

Phil. That was Phil's voice saying his name and speaking to him and it would be Phil's shape when he turned and looked, probably his flickering type of smile with the one eyebrow winced down above it — as if his smiling always hurt. There was no reason to be scared of Phil, no edge in the way that he'd spoken, but Tom found himself curling over slightly under his words, a cold space swinging open in his chest. He listened to the spatter of his pebbles dropping down beside him and wondered why his hands had let go of them. When he breathed, his ribs jumped and he wanted to cough.

'Sorry. Tom? Sorry, man, I thought you knew I was here.'

Feet hurried in a slither over the gravel towards him, close and then closer. Hands settled on his shoulders and something happened.

'Tom? How's stuff, sir? Speak to me.' The hands fastened into a grip and something was changed. 'You set for a cup of tea, maybe? Billy fixed the gas, it's working again. Tom? Come back to me, Tom.'

Phil started another sentence, then sighed it away again,

no more he could say, and Tom felt himself turned softly and held. Phil patted his back, set one palm, cool and still at the base of his neck, eased Tom in tight so he wouldn't fall while he snagged in the last breath he needed before he could cry.

At first, Tom didn't know what it was, the crying. He only felt something snap loose around his heart, like a big spring bursting and a pain in his forehead and a thickness in his mouth. It seemed as if he was trying to get out from inside himself while Phil kept him hugged and steady and thought God knew what – his brother's face running down over his shirt for no good reason at all.

'Come on and we'll sit. Tom? We're heading for the grass over there, sir. If you open your eyes, you'll see.'

Tom lifted his head and bleared out at the bright sky in the water. He noticed a pair of little grey birds with long tails – they had a funny, short way of whistling, as if they were worried over something. Phil was steering him round the waterside, slightly unsteady. They wove and stumbled with their arms round each other's shoulders and from a distance they must look like unfamiliar lovers, or drunks.

An unexpected tussock defeated them both and Tom allowed himself to fall, suddenly as loose and easy as a lamb, as a baby, as mindless elastic. He was surprised when he landed and didn't bounce.

Phil dropped with him, but then broke the contact as

he rolled. He sat up, looking for his cap, found it mashed under one hand, grinned and snugged it back in place.

Tom didn't want to do anything other than lie – a clump of what he guessed were primroses was shining by his face and the grass was very soft here. This was undoubtedly the softest grass he had ever lain in.

'You're going to stay there, then?'

'Uh hu.'

'Well at least you're smiling again.'

'Am I?' Tom had been out of touch with his face, but now he thought about it, he felt as though he was indeed smiling. Phil reached down to nudge him.

'What was all that about? If you don't mind my asking.'

'I don't mind. You got a handkerchief?'

'Not that I'd give it to you. What was it?'

Tom pulled up his sweater in both hands and rubbed his face.

'Unkempt bugger – always were. Tell your Uncle Phil, just between us boys . . .'

'I don't know. I promise. If I knew, I'd tell you – I'd tell anyone around. I mean, it's nothing special, I'm just shaky, jumpy.'

'I'd never have guessed. Shaky or not you're looking well, though.'

'It wouldn't be hard to look better than I did.'

Phil took off his hat again and gripped it while he tipped his face up to the sun.

'I thought you were on the way out that time, you

know. Some state you were in. You were on top of a car when they found you, but they didn't know why.'

'Beats me.'

'I'd have guessed you fell out of a plane from the way you were looking. Some state.'

'That was at the hospital, I remember that bit. Some of it. I was glad you came.'

'Pa would have, but he couldn't. He was worried.'

'Sure.'

'You were the wee one — he always worried about you. He'd be glad to see you now. Your eyes are different.'

'Uh hu.'

'I mean, I don't want to know what you're doing, or how you're doing it, but I hope you keep on. And Pa would, too. So any help you need . . . are you listening?'

Tom was whistling quietly through his teeth, trying not to feel anything else. He knew he would cry again, if he let what his brother was saying reach in to him. Enough was enough, even if he was shaky — he couldn't be crying all the time. He coughed and sat up, pinching a little dampness away from his nose. For a moment, he heard the blood boom in his ears — a definite sign of life as usual. He tapped Phil's hand.

'I am listening. Leave it for a bit, though, eh? And see that bloody hat?'

'What?'

'That ancient fucking monument you've got held in your hands.'

'Mm?'

'Well, here it goes.'

Tom snatched for the cap — a waxy green object, probably as old as he was — and lurched up with it into a run. When he was clear of Phil, he threw the thing in a spin, clean out across the water and felt the day somehow slip out of time as the hat hovered ridiculously, lazy drops of water yawning, aimless, away from it, wherever it sheared the pool. Phil's shout was elongated into something almost musical, all mixed in with the huge, slow rush of Tom's pulse, exploding and exploding.

Then the world fell back to normal while Phil tore at the grass in his scramble to stand, a duck clattered up out of nothing and Tom came to the edge of being afraid again. He couldn't think why he'd done what he'd done, only that it felt good. Phil's face was shouting at him.

'What the hell are you playing at? Crazy fucking bastard. Don't just stand there smiling. That's my hat. Jesus God. That's my outdoors hat, there.'

The cap had landed and was bobbing quietly, its waxiness allowing it to float.

'Uh hu, that'll be it, then. Outdoors.'

'Well, what are you going to do about it?'

'Do about it?'

'Yes, you stupid bastard. What are going to do about it?'

'About it?'

'It!'

'You want a new one?'

'No I do not.'

'You want that one?'

'Well of course I bloody do.'

'OK.'

And it seemed right that Tom should put his hands in his pockets and walk out into the pool, very slowly, easing his way as the shock of the water crept up his legs. It took almost a minute before his feet felt wet.

'What the fuck are you up to now?'

'Getting your hat.'

'Come out of there.'

'No.'

He turned, staggering slightly at the resistance around his legs.

'Come out.'

'No, I'm busy.'

Phil was leaning forward, his fingers twisted together over his stomach in a kind of bunch. He was frowning and wincing and shaking his head. He didn't look especially dangerous, only odd.

'You don't understand. Tom?'

'What?'

'I said, you don't understand. There's a responsibility . . .'

'Can't hear you.'

'Responsibility. With a hat . . . it's like . . .' The frowns had eased now and the whites of his eyes were flaring. There was a tremble in his legs. 'It's like as if you had a pet.' His hands freed each other and lifted to his face. 'Oh, Jesus.'

'Can't hear you.'

Tom felt his stomach tense, wanted to run, but knew that the water would trip him and make him fall. He stared while Phil, still cradling his own head, but also now barking softly with laughter, stepped off to join him in the pool. Phil's legs sunk unevenly and he flailed his arms while he shouted, 'A fucking pet . . . As if it was a pet. Bloody pet hat. I'm as cracked as you. Bloody cracked.'

Tom found himself shouting almost painfully, although his brother was hardly any space away and getting much closer, 'Yes. Cracked. The two of us.'

While they made for the cap together, they could hear themselves laughing and swashing, easing in whimpering breaths, only to howl them all out again. The hat danced off from them a little as they stalked up nearer to it, waist high in the water, chilled senseless.

'You want one, Phil?'

Billy broke his lager open with a liquid hiss. He took a little sip from the can then tapped it down on the folding-table he'd set out for them all in the caravan's biggest room. He was smiling, still wiping the last of the washing-up damp from his forearms.

'You'll be having coffee, Tom?'

It had been meant as a question, Tom knew that, but he felt the words as an order, as something to single him out. He was going to have a mood if he wasn't careful, he could feel one on the way. Perhaps it would be best to get out to the kitchen and look through that window, it had the calmest view – nothing but wet, moving colours and no land, like the pictures his mind could paint when he was happy. He stretched to ease his tension, gain some time. Billy kept on smiling in a way Tom couldn't like. He aimed his voice straight at the smile.

'I'll have some tea and I'll make it.' Now that sounded rude, that sounded as if he was edgy when he really wasn't anything much, except a tiny bit away from himself, constricted. He tried to say, 'Would anyone else like one?' as if it were no kind of threat. Didn't manage.

Phil tried to change the subject, help him out. 'What I would like is to take myself out for a walk, get some air. I don't know how you can stick this, Billy.'

'Well, I'm usually here on my own, so there's too much room for me. Sleep in a different bed every night.' Billy dug in and deepened his grin.

'And you always were the boy for that.' Phil gave a larger than usual wince and tugged his hand through the fine hairs at the crown of his head. He would be bald there, soon, you could tell. 'I meant that we must be something of an imposition.'

'I like the company. All the brothers together. Especially young Tommy, eh?'

'What's that supposed to mean?'

'Just what you'd expect, Tom, just what you'd expect.'

'Well, I'm going for a fucking walk myself now. I'll see you. Phil. Billy.'

Knowing he should take a jacket, knowing he didn't want to go, knowing he ought to say he was sorry and not be the way he was, he pushed past Billy and walked through his brothers' silence to the door. No one would follow him, he felt that. They would let him be cold and on his own and walking for the sake of moving until his brains could settle.

He glanced down and remembered he was wearing trainers because his good shoes were still drying out after the pool. Now he would have to pick his way through the mud. Fuck it, they were clean, his trainers.

The headland track wasn't too bad – an island of grass snaked fairly reliably between the twin channels cut in by occasional tyres. Theirs had been the last car up here – Billy's Cavalier. He kept it nice, his motor, immaculate bodywork and the engine in good nick, too. Usually Tom didn't like to be in cars, it reminded him he couldn't drive any more, wound him up, but Billy made it easier. He had a confident way about him that let you appreciate what he was doing, a natural driver – good tapes playing, an air freshener thing that didn't make the whole place smell like a toilet. Healthy, that's what it was, a healthy car.

A ewe lifted her head and watched him quietly, chewing.

'And fuck you, too.' But he could hear the anger was out of his voice. 'No, that would be fuck ewe, wouldn't it. Geddit? Fuck ewe.' His ears were a little too full of the breeze for him to hear his laugh, because it was only a small one, but he felt it. The ewe twitched an ear and went back to her grass.

Tom pushed both his hands into the pockets of his jeans, beginning to feel the cold. His own fault, shouldn't be out here in the first place, never mind having no coat. If he kept his speed up, he would manage all right, stoke his circulation round, but that was still making the best of a stupid job. Screwed up again.

It wasn't as if he'd expected paradise. The last time he really spoke to Phil and Billy would have been the funeral, maybe five years ago, or six. Somebody told him later he'd punched Billy after the service, but he couldn't remember and Billy had never mentioned it. Looking at it that way, things were going pretty well. Nobody punched so far. Still, he couldn't think why they'd asked him up, why to stay so close together with nothing to do but be inside and stare at each other or be outside and stare at that.

Which was no bad deal. Outside had been very impressive, before they'd come even half of the way. Tom had sat in the front seat, next to Billy, followed the line of the road, and seen and seen until his eyebrows ached. He'd looked at mountains on postcards, calendars, even been up here once before, or somewhere fairly similar, but it had never seemed like this. Now there was nothing between him and all this sight, all this everything with just a little snow flashed high and close under the sky to make it entirely perfect.

'What's up?'

Billy had nudged his attention from a particularly monumental assembly of light and rock.

'Uh?'

'What's the matter, you feel sick, or something?'

'No. I'm fine. Why?'

'Just, you were making these wee noises. Are you an OK boy?'

'Oh, yes.'

'You sounded like a dog having its ears scratched.'

Phil leaned his head forward between the front seats. 'Having its where scratched?'

'Ears. Ears I said and ears I meant. If I'd wanted to say arse, I would have. But as I would have remarked, before I was interrupted, probably our brother is happy. Favourably affected by the view.'

'That right, Tommy?'

'Yes. Yes, that's right.'

Tom remembered being disappointed with himself. Everything he'd said seemed flat when inside he had this big shining feeling that he wanted to turn into good words, or singing, or just some kind of expression, for

God's sake. All he could manage was sounding like a mildly happy dog.

The landscape had calmed down a little until they were almost at the caravan. For a few miles the road had curled between banks and low trees, cosy. Then Billy slowed to a stop.

'OK Tom. You close your eyes now.'

'What?'

'Close your eyes. I did this with Phil the first time he was here, don't worry. It's the best way, you'll thank me. Eh, Phil?'

'Are we that far already? Sure. Sure, you should do it, Tom. We'll not explain, it'll only spoil it, but we're not winding you up, I promise. Go on and close your eyes.'

Billy let the car ease forward and Tom felt a turn and the beginning of a blind descent, everything slightly exaggerated so that he found it reassuring to brace his hands against the dashboard. Their motion smoothed down to nothing again and he heard the handbrake bite, then Phil speaking close to his head.

'A prize for our Tom coming with us. Want to take a look?'

They were perched over the brow of a hill and for half a breath the grey fall of the road drew his eye away to the right. Then he saw, forgot his breathing, drifted beyond his smile.

The valley paused while he blinked down along it, smoke-coloured slopes stepping out in strict perspective on to a dove-blue finger of loch. Like a scene for a shadow play with Balinese curls in the black of the highest pines.

He didn't think he'd known about Balinese curls, but in his mind they appeared to be quite at home here.

A noise broke his attention. It was Phil and Billy, both groaning like happy dogs. Or happy people – they'd been trying to make him feel at home and he'd suddenly found himself noticing what very good men they were and wondering why it hadn't been clear before, and if he should tell them.

'How's that suit you then, sir?'

He'd cleared his throat carefully and heard himself say, 'Not bad, is it?' which made Phil and Billy break out laughing, not being polite or even making fun of him, just big, daft laughter, to do with what he'd said. It was the first time he could remember having really made someone laugh that way which was why he'd been laughing, too, until his vision blurred.

He was beginning to feel content again now, sliding his way over the long twist of indestructible flotsam some high tide had left on the pale shore grass. Plastic from all over the world, maybe – or just across the Sound. Not very romantic, either way. He tried not to let it spoil his mood and lifted his face to the wind that could have rolled in all the miles from America, over the backs of sharks and submarines and undersea cables dreaming.

He was fast exhausting the final yards of land, heading for a tiny buckled jetty, heaped together out of oddly small stones. The whole thing twisted down to nothing like a ruined roof set on the waves. He sprinted the last distance, pushing himself right to the unsteady edge, enjoying the little flutter every move in the loosened cobbles gave his heart. The rocks were bound round with a single strip of rusty metal. There was something brave about that, he liked it.

In any direction, whatever he saw seemed like the end of everything – the grey numbed air, the cold blue suck of the water, or the high, mad spines of stone that raced up out of the grass clear along the promontory as if God had planted a terrible city there and then thought better of it. He shut his eyes and listened, unsteadied, smiling, fractionally hypnotised by the constant boiling hiss at his feet and the buffeting sky. They must have been some people, the ones who lived here, who built the church and raised the cross on the little hill. But he was here now, so he must be some people, too.

The warmth in the caravan was almost shocking, it rushed into his lungs and between his fingers with a kind of sour, friendly damp.

'Is that you, then?' Billy darted his head out from behind the living-room curtain. There was something hesitant about him, enquiring. 'You look cold.'

'Didn't take my jacket, did I? In too much of a hurry. Daft. Sorry.'

'Well, I'll put the kettle on.'

'I can do it.'

'I know you can. But . . .'

Billy moved forward and began to organise his galley; finding, adjusting, spooning, wiping whatever was needed, just so. There was something very comfortable about the way he moved, with now and then a flickered look at Tom.

'Even though you can, I would like to.'

'No, fine. That's fine. You've just been running about, you know — being the housewife for us.'

'But I'm used to that. I have to look after myself all the time. Phil's got Mary and you . . . well, I don't remember you being very domestic.'

'No, I'm not.'

'Then leave it to an expert. I like to be well taken care of, so I always make sure that I am. For you, I . . .'

Bill turned down the hob, studying the wavers in the flame, while his hand reached out and stroked along Tom's cheek. The quick lightness of the touch made him start. Still watching the gas, Bill found Tom's hand and held it.

'Are you better now?'

'I . . . don't know.'

'Are you better now?'

'I'm happy.'

'Are you better now?'

'There's stuff, things I don't have to do any more. I mean, I'm just happy.'

Billy turned.

'You're happy.'

'Uh hu.'

'Sorry about the lager.'

'It's OK.'

'It so happens that there isn't any more. We're what you might call a dry house now.'

'You know what, Billy?'

'No, what?'

'You've got green eyes.'

Tom felt his hand gripped tighter and then softly let fall.

'I've always had green eyes. They're one of my best points. Did you never look before?'

'I suppose not. I might have forgotten.'

The kettle squealed quietly while Bill shook his head, 'Well, now that you're back, Tom, will you join me in a cup of tea?'

There was something pleasantly clumsy about their preparations for the night. They were turning in early, the comfortable heat of the gas fire and the still dark muffling the windows seemed to have slowed them all down to a stop. They yawned and stretched and snuffled, abandoned their final card game in an easy muddle. Tom had first turn for the bathroom.

'On you go, Tom. You're the visitor – you don't want to have to follow Phil to the sink. The man is a pig.'

'You've been living on your own too long, that's your trouble. Chuck us another biscuit, Bill, before I have to clean my teeth. And mind you put your sterile gloves on, Tom – Bill here is on the surgical side of houseproud.'

'Like I say – a pig.'

The caravan rocked as he shuffled along the passageway, cautious in his second best socks. Once he'd agreed to come up here he'd bought a sponge bag and a soap dish and a towel, even pyjamas, for fuck's sake – in a panic because he had nothing to go away with. They would have lent him gear, but that wasn't the point, he should have his own. Everything was rolled together now in a bundle under his arm, all his.

He could hear Phil and Billy, still happily bickering, as he snibbed shut the bathroom door and surrendered himself to the cold. He filled the sink with the hottest water the tap could manage and shuddered and scrubbed and shuddered, splashing the carpet and awkward – banged his arm.

He felt better once the pyjamas were on and his sweater over the top, the softness of flannel and the dry smell of new cloth. Peering through the water steam and the flurry of his own breath, he watched himself lather his face with new shaving soap and begin easy, easy strokes with a new razor. He couldn't have waited till morning to try it out.

For a moment in the cloudy mirror he could see his face young. He had the memory of his mother begging and harrying all of them into bed and safe out of the way. When Pa came home they had to be asleep, they must be sleeping. He felt himself lying frozen with his eyes shut, hoping there would be no voices in that paper-walled house, hoping for no noises, no crying and no footsteps suddenly storming to turn on their light. When he was a boy he'd always been hoping.

He finished the shave and towelled his cheeks, checked in the mirror — not exactly a boy, but not in bad shape. And another day almost over, made it again, that deserved a smile.

Tom woke into a numb dark, silent and absolute. He forgot where he was, forgot the caravan and its shape, and could find nothing to help him in the windowless black. He lay sweating inside his sleeping bag as the last of his nightmare tipped down over him like a scream.

Rolling and fighting to free his limbs, he dropped from the bunk to the box room floor and stunned himself fully awake. He sat for a time he could not later measure, opening and closing his eyes and finding no difference in what he could see, but trying all the time to think. He was afraid of something he didn't know, also of dying and of falling asleep.

In the end, he unzipped the sleeping bag and wrapped it around his shoulders, stood up and calmed himself enough to open his door. Afraid of the dark — that was no use. He had to be firm with himself, there, and trust there was no reason for the fear.

Once he was moving down the passage, he felt more normal. Outside a night-time animal called and made the world a little more convincing before he eased back the curtain on the big room. It was still slightly warm in there. A dim shape moved to his left.

'What's up?'

'Sorry.'

'What's the matter? And mind Billy, he's on the floor.'

'Eh? Oh. Sorry, I didn't know – '

'It's all right, Phil, he knows where I am now.'

'Couldn't you sleep, sir?'

'I slept, but I woke up. I had a dream.'

'We heard.'

'Well, I'm going for a piss now I'm awake. Mind out, Tommy, I think you're still standing on something of mine.'

'Sorry, Bill.' A dim blur coughed past him. 'Um . . . sorry.'

'Don't just stand there whispering sorry, sir, get some kip.'

'I know, but . . .'

'OK, OK. Wait until Bill gets back and we'll sort something out.'

'I feel a right idiot.'

'So what's new?'

They were all shivering by the time they finished the

arrangements and turned off the lamp again. Tom had been slightly wary at the feel of his sleeping bag, tight against his shoulders, but then the warmth of his own self gathering around him seemed to help him relax. He almost felt drowsy. Phil and Billy were settling themselves, one on either side of him – all the brothers uncomfortable together on the floor. Phil sat up and punched the cushion wedged under his legs.

'God's sake. Here we are, then. Just like the fucking Waltons. Well good night brother Billy and good night brother Tom. Try and sleep, eh? Or we'll kill you.'

Billy wriggled. 'Sush, Phil, I was nearly away then. Goodnight all. And take it easy, Tom. Tom?'

'Tom?'

'I'm sorry, I . . .'

Phil twisted round in the dark.

'Shut up. We're here and it's all right now. It's all right.'